Puffin Plus
The Intruder

It was dusk, and the tide was coming in. The thin, narrow-faced stranger asked sixteen-year-old Arnold to guide him over the miles of dangerous sands. When they were far from land, he called the boy across to him.

'What did you say your name was?'

'Arnold Haithwaite.'

The stranger pulled a flashlight from his raincoat pocket and shone it suddenly in Arnold's face.

'You can't be Arnold Haithwaite,' he said. 'Because *I'm* Arnold Haithwaite.'

'You're daft,' said Arnold. He thought it was a joke, and not very funny. But the stranger was no harmless eccentric. When they came to tread through the river, running out between sandbanks to the sea, Arnold felt himself grabbed from behind and pulled backwards into the water.

It was the start of Arnold's fight against a threat to his identity, perhaps to his life. Peter and Jane, whose father was helping to build the nuclear power station down the coast, did their best to help Arnold. But in the end there was only one way the menace could be defeated ...

This story, with its fierce, wild setting in an estuary where the tide comes in like a galloping horse, was made into an award-winning television serial.

Also published in Puffin Plus: *Noah's Castle* and *A Foreign Affair*. And in Puffins, *Dan Alone*, *Gumble's Yard*, *Good-bye to Gumble's Yard*, *Hell's Edge* and *The Islanders*.

The Intruder

John Rowe Townsend
Illustrated by Graham Humphreys

PUFFIN BOOKS
in association with Oxford University Press

Puffin Books, Penguin Books Ltd, Harmondsworth, Middlesex, England
Viking Penguin Inc., 40 West 23rd Street, New York, New York 10010, U.S.A.
Penguin Books Australia Ltd, Ringwood, Victoria, Australia
Penguin Books Canada Ltd, 2801 John Street, Markham, Ontario, Canada L3R 1B4
Penguin Books (N.Z.) Ltd, 182–190 Wairau Road, Auckland 10, New Zealand

First published by Oxford University Press 1969
Published in Peacock Books 1977
Reissued in Puffin Books 1981
Reprinted 1982, 1985

Printed and bound in Great Britain by
Cox & Wyman Ltd, Reading
Set in Linotype Juliana

For Vera

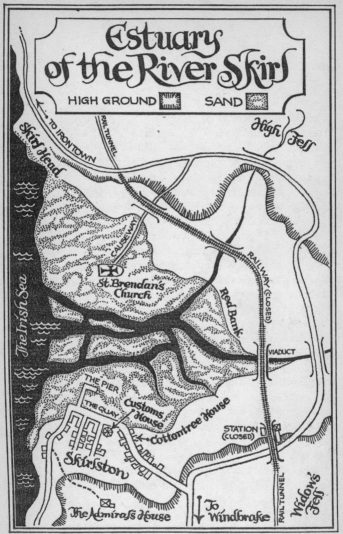

Estuary
of the River Skirl

HIGH GROUND   SAND

The Irish Sea

Skirl Head

TO IRONTOWN

RAIL TUNNEL

High Fell

CAUSEWAY

St. Brendan's Church

Red Bank

RAILWAY (CLOSED)

VIADUCT

THE PIER

THE QUAY

Customs House

Cottontree House

STATION (CLOSED)

Skirlston

RAIL TUNNEL

Widow's Fell

The Admiral's House

To Windbrake

J.A. PHELAN

Chapter One

Sea, sand, stone, slate, sky.

The village is Skirlston. The bay is Skirl Bay. The sands are Skirl Sands. The headland is Skirl Head. All take their names from the River Skirl – a short, fast-flowing stream that starts a bare ten miles away on the western slopes of the Lake District and collects a dozen other streams on its brisk way down to sea.

The village is grey and has dwindled. Once it was a Roman port. It thrived in the Middle Ages and in Tudor times. It thrived above all in the eighteenth century, when the ships from the West Indies brought sugar and rum and raw cotton and tobacco, and the handsome octagonal custom-house was built.

The Skirl made Skirlston and the Skirl unmade it. In the spring floods of 1792 the river changed course in its wide estuary, and thenceforth flowed uselessly to sea a mile away. No ship came again. The bay has silted and silted, the sands have spread ever farther, and Skirlston Quay stands high and dry, except when the spring tides come.

Across the bay from Skirlston is St Brendan's Church, the Church in the Sea. The church is a thousand years old. It has long been deconsecrated and deserted. Once it was on an island. Now sand surrounds it, except when the spring tides come.

The village is grey and has dwindled. The sea has left it, except when the spring tides come. But the winds are strong from the west, and carry spray. On the fells above Skirlston sheep roam, and the stunted trees lean hard to landward.

Sea, sand, stone, slate, sky. That is the landscape.

Chapter Two

Arnold saw the boy and girl a few minutes before he saw the stranger.

Arnold was sitting on the bench outside the Sea Church, eating his sandwiches and counting the tips he had got for guiding a party over the sands. For the time being he was Sand Pilot. The Sand Pilot was responsible for people's safety.

That was why he watched the boy and girl. They were well out to seaward. The sun was going down, and their tiny figures were black against a marmalade sky. They were wearing shorts, and they were playing with a ball, throwing high catches to each other. As often as not, one of them would miss it and the ball would escape across the sands: bounce, bounce, bounce and run. Then it would be recovered and thrown high in the air, and before long it would get away again: bounce, bounce, bounce and run. And all the time they were moving farther from the shore.

They couldn't see the sea. Arnold could see it, because on Church Island he was higher up. The sea was a golden glint, two or three miles away. That was no distance. The sea went out for seven miles or more. But the sea came back. The sea was coming back now. It wouldn't come to the village, it wouldn't come to the church, but it would come to where the boy and girl were. It wouldn't come with a rush. It would rise in the river-bed and the gullies and they wouldn't see it. One minute there'd be sand all round them, the next minute they'd be far out at sea.

There wasn't any danger. Today it would hardly come above their knees. But sometimes people took fright and ran the wrong way and stumbled into the river-mouth, where the water was deeper and the currents strong.

Arnold cupped his hands and hallooed.

The wind was against his voice and they didn't hear. He hallooed again, more loudly. Now one of them heard – the boy – and waved. His cooee came back to Arnold on the breeze. But he hadn't understood. The ball soared high, the girl missed it. Bounce, bounce, bounce and run.

'Come back!' Arnold called.

Another wave from the boy, and the ball flew up again.

'Come back!' yelled Arnold.

The stranger coughed just behind him. Arnold, watching the two figures on the sands, hadn't seen him come over the causeway from the mainland at the bay's north side. He was close, uncomfortably close. When Arnold turned round their faces were inches apart.

'Youngsters haven't much sense these days,' the man said.

Arnold turned again, cupped his hands, shouted once more at the top of his voice:

'Come back!'

'Daft,' said the stranger. 'That's what they are. Daft.'

'No dafter than most,' said Arnold. 'They don't know, that's all. Folk don't, till they're told.'

The boy and girl showed no sign of having heard him. But they had stopped skying the ball. They were throwing it at shoulder height between them, trotting now towards Skirlston. Arnold was relieved.

'A bit far out,' he said, 'but they'll be all right if they keep on that way.'

Colour was fading from the sky. It would soon be dusk. Arnold could just make out the stranger's appearance. He was thin, getting towards middle age, and he wore a shabby raincoat, and a black beret square on the head. His face was narrow, and even in this light you could see that there was something odd about his eyes. One moved, the other stayed still. His voice was sharp, northern, slightly abrasive.

'I want to be in Skirlston tonight,' he said.

'So do I,' said Arnold shortly. He crammed what were left of his sandwiches into his haversack, took up the Sand Pilot's staff. His mind was still on the two figures he had seen, now nearly out of sight but still heading for Skirlston. He scrambled down from

Church Island to the sand. The stranger followed, picking his way gingerly from rock to rock.

'You'll know these sands well, I reckon?' he said.

'I do that. I'm the Sand Pilot now. Or as good as.'

'You won't mind if I come with you?'

'Please yourself,' said Arnold. He looked down at the stranger's feet.

'You'll ruin your shoes,' he said. 'If I was you I'd go back over the causeway and up to the main road and get a bus.'

The man didn't go back. He walked beside Arnold in silence for a minute. Then he said, slowly:

'I don't like being told what to do.'

'I wasn't telling you,' Arnold said. 'Just suggesting.'

'And what did you say you were?' the man asked.

'The Sand Pilot. Well, sort of. The real Sand Pilot's the Admiral. That's Joe Hardwick. But he's not too good these days. I do it for him mostly. Guiding parties over the bay and watching that folk don't come to harm.'

'You've got a big job on,' the man said. He sounded impressed. 'A responsible job for a lad. Let's see, how old would you be?'

'Sixteen, just.'

'I might be able to use a lad like you.'

Arnold said nothing.

'I'm a businessman, you know. You might not think it, to look at me.'

Arnold still said nothing.

'You think of a businessman as having a bowler hat and a brief-case and all that, don't you?'

'I don't know,' said Arnold. He didn't think of businessmen at all. He didn't know any – unless you counted Len Crowther at the smithy, who owned the village petrol pump and drove the school taxi and dealt in sheep and chickens and took fish to Irontown market.

'Well, I'm a businessman. Not in a big way yet. Just starting, in fact, you might say. But with a future. And there could be an opening for a bright lad.'

'Keep moving,' said Arnold. 'You can feel the sand softening. That means the tide's on its way.'

'I'm staying in Skirlston tonight,' the stranger said.

Arnold was only half listening. The boy and girl were in his mind still. They weren't local. Locals only went on the sand for shrimping or to stake their nets for flat-fish. And he didn't think they were tourists. Tourists hardly came to Skirlston except for the sand crossing. Perhaps they belonged to the family that was moving in with old Miss Hendry.

A boy and girl in shorts, and a ball thrown high against the sun. Something about the sight had intrigued and disturbed him. They were far away by now, were probably back in Skirlston.

'I'm at the house with the funny tree,' the stranger went on.

That made Arnold attend.

'The cotton tree,' he said. 'That's *my* house.'

'There's a queer old chap there. I had quite a talk with him.'

'My dad.'

'I'd have thought he was a bit old to be your dad.'

'Well, maybe,' said Arnold. 'I call him Dad. I've always lived there.'

'And what's your name, son?'

'Arnold Haithwaite.'

'Arnold what?'

'Haithwaite.'

They walked on for two or three minutes in silence. Arnold prodded the sand from time to time. There weren't any quick-sands here, but the texture helped him to tell where the tide had got to.

'Don't be scared if it's round your feet in a few minutes,' he said. 'I told you you'd get your shoes wet.'

But now it was the stranger who didn't seem to be listening. He plodded on with his head down.

'You're all right, are you?' asked Arnold after a minute or two

'Oh yes, I'm all right. W*hat* did you say your name was?'

'Arnold Haithwaite,' said Arnold again.

'And the old chap. What's *his* name?'

'Ernest Haithwaite.'

The man stood still.

'Come here!' he said.

Arnold went close to him. It was dark now. The stranger pulled a flashlight from his raincoat pocket and shone it suddenly in Arnold's face, making him blink.

'You can't be Arnold Haithwaite,' he said. 'Because I'm Arnold Haithwaite.'

'You're daft,' said Arnold. He moved on. There was time to get to Skirlston and twenty minutes to spare, but you didn't linger on these sands.

The man laughed aloud.

'I assure you I'm Arnold Haithwaite,' he said in a thin, assertive tone.

'If it's a joke,' said Arnold, 'it's not all that funny. Now listen, we're just going to cross the river. If your shoes are still dry you might as well take them off. Tie them together and hold them in one hand. And roll your trousers well up.'

'You're not taking any notice,' the man said. 'I just told you something.'

'And I'm telling you something,' said Arnold. 'I'm telling you to watch your step. It's wide and shallow here, but it's quick-flowing and you can easy slip.'

'I like folk to listen to me,' said the stranger. 'I get cross when folk don't listen.'

'Oh, give up,' said Arnold, 'and come along. Look, seeing it's dark we'll link arms. I don't want you going over.'

Arm in arm they trod through the River Skirl. The first channel was shallow, the second was deeper, the third rose quickly to knee height. Arnold, as always down here, was wearing sandals and khaki ex-Army shorts. The man hadn't done anything about his shoes and trousers. His legs were getting soaked.

'This is the worst bit,' Arnold said. 'You'll be through in a minute. Now we've got to get up on to that brack.'

A sandbank rose eighteen inches above the river's surface.

'It's hanging over a bit,' Arnold said. 'First time I set foot on it, it'll fall in. Second time should be all right. I'll go first and give you a hand.'

He had judged it correctly. Yards of sand along the edge of the bank crumbled into the water. But once the overhang had gone the bank held him, though his feet sank into it.

Arnold was almost at the top when he felt himself grabbed from behind, and fell backwards into the water. He took a deep mouthful before he knew what was happening. And then he was struggling with the stranger. He was in the water, out of the water, on top at one moment, then being held below. The stranger's hand was on his face. He was drowning . . . Arnold made a huge effort, turned and twisted, found a footing in the river-bed, pushed the man away and swung round to face him. Arnold was solid and strong, but he hadn't the muscular development, the sudden power of a man.

But the stranger didn't attack again. He stood a few feet away, silent. Arnold spluttered and spat out water.

'What happened?' the man asked. He sounded surprised.

'You tell *me* what happened!' said Arnold, furious. 'You . . . you tried to kill me!'

'Nay,' the man said. 'I lost my nerve for a second, that was all.'

'I don't believe you. Nobody in his senses would grab from behind like that. And you were trying to hold me down.'

Arnold and the stranger were both standing in the water, dripping wet. Cautiously, without taking his eyes from the man, Arnold backed to the river's edge. He retrieved his staff, stuck at an angle in the sandbank, and waved it in the air.

'You keep your distance this time!' he said. And in a flurry of wet sand he scrambled from the river. The man made no move.

Arnold trotted towards Skirlston. There was one more shallow channel, and he crossed it without breaking step. Then it was level going all the way.

The man had emerged from the river and now followed him, staying twenty or thirty yards behind. Arnold broke into a run. The stranger increased his speed to match, and kept the same distance. Arnold stood still and made a threatening gesture with the staff. The man stood still. Arnold trotted again and the man trotted.

After five minutes they were above the tide-line. The last half mile to Skirlston Quay was over dry powdery sand, bad for running. Arnold lumbered across it, picking up his feet with difficulty. Just under the quay the man caught up.

'Get back!' Arnold warned him.

'Here, listen to me a minute.'

'I don't want to listen to you. I reckon you're barmy or something. I'm going up to see Fred Bateman at the police house.'

'Don't be hasty, lad. I didn't mean you any harm.'

They faced each other, ten feet apart, with Skirlston Quay looming above. Nobody was about. Arnold didn't like the thought of a struggle on the narrow, unguarded stone steps that went up the side of the quay.

'Of course you meant harm,' he said. 'You were trying to drown me.'

'I thought you were trying to drown *me*,' the man said.

Arnold was astounded.

'Who grabbed who?' he demanded.

'All right, I grabbed hold of you. I'm sorry, it was a mistake. I was just scared for a second, like I said. I'd have let you go quicker if you hadn't fought. I didn't know what was happening myself.'

Arnold stared at him through the gloom, still unbelieving. It was too dark now to read anything from his face.

'Why did you say you were Arnold Haithwaite?' he asked at length.

'Just a joke, son.'

'I'm not laughing,' said Arnold.

'All right, all right.' The stranger sounded impatient now, his voice sharper. 'Let's not stand here arguing. Show me how we get off this beach.'

'We go up these steps,' said Arnold, 'and you can go first. And you can tell me who you really are.'

'There'll be time for that when we get to the house.'

'You really are staying the night at Cottontree House?' Arnold asked.

'I told you so, didn't I? Don't you like the idea?'

'No.'

'Come now, lad, you're getting all the wrong ideas. Seeing we're going to be under the same roof we might as well be pals, mightn't we? Shake.'

He came closer. Arnold recoiled a step. The stranger's hand was thrust forward. Warily Arnold took it. It gripped him hard and long. Arnold clenched his other fist, suspecting for a moment some trickery. But the stranger released him.

'There,' he said. 'Now we've met officially. I dare say we'll meet a good deal more.'

He ran lightly up the steps ahead of Arnold, the wet trousers flapping round his legs.

Chapter Three

The cotton tree grew up the front of the house and threw out a long branch sideways below the upstairs windows. Experts said it was really a kapok. Its seed had come from the Indies. Its trunk was thick and grey, wonderfully gnarled and whorled. Its leaves kept the front rooms dark, all summer through. The cotton tree was two hundred years old, and the house perhaps half a century older – a square grey-stone house between village street and fore-shore.

Over the downstairs window an ancient signboard, just legible, said GENERAL STORE. In the front of the same window were brown-edged cards saying TEAS and BED & BREAKFAST and VACANCIES. They had been there since before Agnes Haithwaite died, six years ago.

Arnold reached Cottontree House ten minutes after the stranger. He had had some nets to collect from the railings of Skirlston Quay. He put them in the outhouse, thought briefly of going farther up the street for a word with Fred Bateman the policeman, decided against it and went in at the back door. In the kitchen, in a rocking-chair, Ernest Haithwaite dozed in the fug from a great fire. He opened his eyes as Arnold went in, closed them again, said nothing. Arnold put the kettle on, made tea, poured two cups, mended the fire, ate the rest of his sandwiches. Then he dug the old man in the ribs and pointed to the cooling tea. Ernest Haithwaite, humped in a corner of his chair, held the cup between his hands and sipped, rocking slowly. Still no word was said. Sometimes no word was said all evening. Ernest had stories to tell of old times, and liked to tell them, but Arnold had heard them often enough already.

Ernest Haithwaite was a small man whose clothes now seemed a size too big for him. His features, always craggy, were sharpening

with age. His hair, once plentiful, was thinning and grizzled. He shaved every Sunday, and sometimes during the week as well.

The old man was putting his cup down when a tap came on the door that led to the main house. He struggled to get up. Arnold waved him down, handed him his false teeth from the mantelpiece.

'There's a feller staying the night,' the old man said.

'I know,' said Arnold.

The tap came again before he could get to the door. The stranger put his head round.

'Nice and cosy in here,' he said.

'There's a sitting-room for visitors along the passage,' said Arnold.

'It's cold and gloomy, that place is,' the stranger said. 'Like a morgue. I wouldn't be surprised if it was a bit damp, too.'

'You needn't stay if you don't want,' said Arnold. 'You'll get a room at the Hendry Arms, most likely.'

'Now, lad,' the old man protested. 'That doesn't sound like you.' He turned to the stranger. 'You can come in if you like, mister. Come in and have a sit-down. You look wet. What you been doing?'

'He's been playing on the sands,' said Arnold grimly.

The stranger ignored him.

'You'll be Mr Ernest Haithwaite,' he said to the old man. 'I didn't realize that when I was speaking to you before.'

'That's right,' Ernest said.

'I was telling your lad,' said the stranger, 'that I wouldn't be surprised if we was related.'

'Oh aye?' said Ernest. He spoke without much interest. But Arnold stared.

'You said . . .' he began. And then, to the old man:

'He told me he was Arnold Haithwaite. And then he said it was a joke.'

The old man looked slightly bewildered, but still not much concerned.

'Be that as it may,' the stranger said. One eye roved round the room. The other stayed disconcertingly still. 'Be that as it may, there's lots of Haithwaites in my family. Let's see, where do your folks come from? Are they local?'

'Local?' said Ernest. 'Local? I should say they're local. There's been Haithwaites in Skirlston for two hundred years past. Or three or four or five hundred for all I know. I been here nearly eighty myself, though you might not think so from looking at me. I used to work on the railway here. Fifty years I worked on the railway, till they closed this line down. Back in nineteen-thirteen I started, when I was only a lad. I could tell you some tales of those days . . .'

'I bet you could,' the stranger said. 'Are *all* your family in Skirlston?'

'I've got no family now to speak of,' said the old man. 'My son Frank died ten years ago. Then it was my wife, six years back.' He sighed. 'Now there's only me and Arnold. I used to have some cousins in Cobchester, mind you, but I never hear from them now.'

'In Cobchester, eh?' The stranger sounded surprised and excited. 'You did say Cobchester?'

'Aye, I said Cobchester. What's so funny about that? Plenty of folks come from Cobchester. It's the biggest place in the north-west, after all.'

'My family are from Cobchester, too,' the stranger said. 'Would you believe it?'

'No,' said Arnold. Again the man ignored him and spoke to Ernest.

'What part of Cobchester are your folks from?

'Claypits, when last I heard of them,' the old man said.

'Claypits! There you are. Amazing. We're from Claypits as well.'

'Oh aye?' said Ernest. At his time of life it took a lot to arouse his interest.

'What were your cousins' names?' the stranger asked.

'Let's see. There was Elsie, that married Albert Sutcliffe, and Ada, that never got wed at all, and Tom. Tom Haithwaite. I didn't see him again after the first war . . .'

The stranger got up, went over to the old man and shook his hand.

'Uncle!' he said. 'Uncle Ernest! I'm Tom Haithwaite's son. Your nephew! Elsie and Ada was my aunties.'

'Tom's been dead thirty years.'

'Aye. Very sad,' said the stranger. 'I was only a lad when my dad died.' He sighed.

'He was never married that I know of,' said Ernest.

'He kept it dark,' the stranger said. 'Even from his own family. There was a bit of opposition, like. But he was married all right. And I was his only son.'

'Then your name is Haithwaite?' said Arnold.

'Y I'll write it down for you. Bring me the visitors' book. You have a visitors' book, haven't you? Every place that takes people in should have a visitors' book.'

'Where's the visitors' book, Dad?' Arnold asked.

'Look in that sideboard in the dining-room.'

Arnold got up, went slowly through to the dining-room, and found the visitors' book where the old man had said it was. The last entry was eighteen months ago. There weren't many visitors these days, and the few who came didn't get asked to sign. He took the book to the stranger. The man turned the page, so as to start a fresh leaf. He took a ballpoint from his pocket, wrote the date and then, laboriously but with a flourish:

'Mr Arnold Haithwaite, Claypits, Cobchester 15.'

'There you are,' he said. 'Now are you satisfied?'

'But you told me it was a joke.'

'That was a joke itself.'

'Listen,' said Arnold. 'None of this proves anything at all.' A conviction was growing in his mind.

'I reckon you're a liar,' he said slowly. 'I don't know what you're up to, but you're a liar. Whoever you are, you're not Arnold Haithwaite, because I am. And you tried to drag me down in the water. I reckon you tried to drown me.'

The stranger laughed.

'Come, come,' he said. 'That's not the way to talk to your cousin. Is it, Uncle?'

The old man was baffled.

'You're not telling me there's *two* Arnold Haithwaites?' he said.

'Looks like it,' said the stranger. 'But you can call me Sonny. Most folks call me Sonny.'

'You're a liar,' said Arnold again, his voice rising. 'And you did try to drown me.'

'If I was lying,' the stranger said, 'how would I know all about the Haithwaite family, and coming from Claypits, and my dad being Uncle's cousin?'

'That's right,' said the old man to Arnold. 'He wouldn't, would he?'

'I never heard anything like it,' said the stranger. 'All this about being liars and drowning. Are you out of your senses, lad? It's time you took a grip on things. You could do to learn some manners as well.'

'The lad's not hisself at all tonight,' said Ernest apologetically.

'If I'm to be myself,' said Arnold, 'isn't it time you told me who I am? I've asked you two or three times, and you never tell me anything.'

'All in good time,' the old man said. 'You're still only a lad, though you seem to forget it the way you carry on. I'll tell you it all when the day comes, and you can let that satisfy you for now.'

'You'll be dead when the day comes,' said Arnold.

'Now, now, lad!' the stranger said reprovingly. 'Talking like that to him that's given you a good home all these years! I'm surprised at you. And a very nice place it is, Uncle. I suppose the house is your own property, eh?'

'It belongs to the Duchy of Furness.'

'Oh,' said the stranger. He sounded disappointed.

'It's on lease,' the old man went on. 'Like the rest of Skirlston. The rents are all the same. A bunch of wild violets every year on Lady Day. And the Duchy lets tenants transfer their leases. And you can sell a Duchy lease for a lot of money. So I suppose you could say that to all intents and purposes it's my house.'

'That's better!' the stranger said.

There was something in his voice that irritated Ernest Haithwaite.

'Better for who?' he asked.

'Better for you of course, Uncle.'

'Aye. For me, and for Arnold after me,' the old man said. He was still irritated. 'And don't you be getting any wrong ideas. Arnold's been with me ever since he was a baby. We get along all right and we know each other. He's all the family I've got.'

'Not now, he isn't!' said the stranger quickly. 'You've got me as well, Uncle.'

But the old man was tiring. He didn't often talk so much in the evening. And it was all rather puzzling. He wished none of this had cropped up.

'It's all very well calling me uncle,' he said. 'Seems to me you're some kind of cousin if you're anything. But it's many a long year since I heard from any of the Cobchester lot, and I can't be bothered now. I've had enough of it, if you want to know. I'll be glad when you've gone back to Cobchester.'

The stranger wasn't pleased.

'Oh well, if that's how you feel,' he said, his voice thinner and sharper, 'I'll be leaving you. I thought you'd have been glad to meet another Haithwaite, that's all.'

He got up and stood for a moment in front of Arnold. The one mobile eye fixed itself on the boy's face, square and solid, with dark eyes and complexion and dark curly hair.

'He's not a bit like *you*, is he?' he said to the old man.

'Can't you mind your own business?' said Arnold.

'Oh, I can mind my own business,' the man said. 'I'm good at that.' He half smiled. 'Well, good night, Uncle. And in case I don't see you in the morning, good-bye. But I will be seeing you again, I promise you. There's nothing surer than that.'

He was gone.

The old man looked at Arnold.

'Well!' he said. 'That's a funny state of affairs.'

'Not so funny,' said Arnold.

Ernest Haithwaite could feel that the calm between them had been disturbed.

'You don't want to worry about that feller,' he said. 'He'll be off first thing in the morning and we won't see him again. My family haven't bothered about me for fifty years and I reckon they're not going to start now.'

Arnold was silent. The old man took a pipe from the mantelpiece, knocked the dottle out of it and scraped at the blackened bowl with a penknife.

'Quite a day it's been,' he said. 'I was almost forgetting, among all this, that the new folks have come to Hendrys' place.'

'Oh,' said Arnold, only half attending.

'The man's at the Atomic,' said Ernest. 'There's him and his wife – very smart. And two youngsters, no more than your age, if that.'

'A boy and a girl?' Arnold asked. He recalled the two figures he had seen on the sands. Black against the sunset, throwing a ball. Bounce, bounce, bounce and run. His interest was stirred for a moment.

'Dunno,' said the old man. He had no more to add on the subject. He drew out his pouch and started cutting the thick plug tobacco. The customary silence returned.

' 'Night, Dad,' said Arnold after a few minutes, and left the old man thickening the fuggy air with tobacco smoke. He went to his room, undressed to his shirt and got into bed. Then he got out again and laboriously pushed a huge heavy dresser against the door. He put the bed next to the dresser. He went to the window and looked out at the cotton tree. He could scramble down it and be away in a few seconds if he had to. But somebody from outside could climb up it almost as quickly. Arnold shut the window and jammed it with a piece of wood.

Normally he slept well and never dreamed. Tonight he was uneasy, lay awake for some time, and slept in fits, with fragmentary dreams of which he remembered nothing except that they were full of menace.

He would have known if the door of his room had moved half an inch, but it didn't. And nothing touched his window but the scraping twigs of the cotton tree. The sounds of the night were the hundred different and usual ones set off by the endless Skirlston wind.

Chapter Four

The day Arnold met the stranger, the Ellisons moved into Skirlston Manor. John and Helen Ellison, Peter and Jane.

John Ellison came to Skirlston because he was chief construction engineer for the nuclear power-station, now growing in concrete at Windbrake, five miles down the coast. He rented the manor-house furnished, from the Hendry family, who had gone to live in the Channel Islands and save income tax. He rented it all but the Wing – two rooms and a kitchen – where Aunt Katharine lived. There had been Hendrys in Skirlston for five hundred years, and now there was only Aunt Katharine. She said she wouldn't leave for the Inland Revenue or anyone else.

The Ellisons moved into Skirlston Manor. John and Helen Ellison, Peter and Jane. For the two young Ellisons it wasn't much of an upheaval. They had moved more than once before and they'd move more than once again. It didn't bother them. They were both away at school for most of the year, anyway.

On the day they arrived they ran miles out into the bay, throwing a ball between them, bounce, bounce, bounce and run. They saw and heard nobody, except someone who called a half-heard greeting from the strange, sand-islanded church. On the morning after, they walked down to Skirlston Quay and sat on the one wooden bench that commemorated the coronation of Queen Elizabeth II. They sat looking out across the sands to Skirl Head. The two young Ellisons, Peter and Jane, thirteen and fifteen.

Peter was quick. Everyone knew Peter was quick. He knew it himself. Quick to think, quick to act, restless, bright, top of the class, that was Peter. Quick with his fingers, quick at games, a runner of rings round all in sight. He finished people's sentences for them, got to the end before they did. Quick, quick, quick. That was Peter.

Jane was calm and quiet. Helen Ellison's friends often congratulated her on her daughter. What a lovely girl Jane was, they used to say. Relaxed, no awkwardness about her. Happy with her looks, happy (it seemed) with herself, growing up smoothly. She wasn't snappy or sulky or childish, much. But remote; you couldn't get near her. Wherever you came in getting to know Jane, her self was a step beyond. Peter came nearest, could penetrate brightly and sharply, could strike a spark of response where others failed. For brother and sister they were close, closer than most. Calm, content (it seemed) and remote, that was Jane.

It was a clear blue day in July, but it wasn't warm. The cool west Skirlston wind funnelled in from the sea between headlands and fells. It blew their hair about, made them laugh and shiver. They were thinking of going down to run on the sands when the man came along and tried to start the car.

He came out of Cottontree House. He was thin and shabby. He wore a black beret and carried a fibre suitcase. He stepped along smartly to the open space, behind Peter and Jane and beside the old custom-house, where his elderly black saloon was parked.

The man unlocked his car and got into it and pressed the starter. The engine turned over wearily but didn't fire. The man tried again, and there was only a groan. A few seconds later there was another, diminishing, groan.

The man got out with a starting-handle in his hand. He went to the front of the car and cranked it. Still nothing happened.

Peter went across and offered to help.

'I'm all right, thank you,' the man said. There were no thanks in his tone of voice. He took off his jacket, put it on a low wall near by and rolled up his sleeves. He cranked and cranked, without result.

The man paused and took two or three deep breaths. Then he attacked again, cranking ferociously, as if pitting his strength against an enemy. He kept it up, with enormous effort, for at least a minute. At last, his face red, he gave up, staggered to the low wall and sank on it exhausted.

'You'd better let me have a look,' Peter said. This time the man said nothing.

Peter went across, peered in at the car window.

'The ignition light's showing all right,' he said. 'You should be able to get a spark.'

He lifted the bonnet.

'But the tops of your plugs look damp and dirty to me,' he said. 'That won't help.' He took out a tissue, wiped the plugs, dropped the bonnet, went back to the stranger.

'Try again now,' he suggested.

The man cranked fiercely again, without success.

'*That's* not done much good,' he complained.

It was then that Arnold came along, on his way to the Admiral's. Arnold was whistling because it was a blue day and the fears of the night had gone and the stranger had left Cottontree House and the tide had brought a good catch of flat-fish into his overnight nets. Arnold saw the boy and girl, and knew they were the two he had seen yesterday. Then he saw the man. His whistle hesitated and stopped.

'Is there a garage round here?' Peter asked him. The stranger had slumped on to the wall, breathing hard and saying nothing.

'There's Len Crowther's,' Arnold said. 'But Len's not there now. Gone to Irontown. Then I reckon he'll be over to Harker's farm, up on the pass. He won't be back till dinner.'

The man stood up. Arnold scowled. The man scowled too.

'We could try pushing it,' Peter suggested. 'It might be something that'd clear itself, like a spot of dirt in the carburettor.'

'*You* could try minding your own business,' the man said.

'Oh well, if that's how you feel . . .' said Peter huffily.

'Nay, don't be so hasty,' said the stranger. 'Just listen to me a minute. How old are you, young man?'

'Thirteen.'

'Is it for you to tell older folks what to do?'

'I only wanted to help,' Peter said.

'All right. Well, remember, there's a right way and a wrong way of doing things. Some folk don't like being told. *I* don't like being told. I don't like it at all.'

'I'll remember,' said Peter. 'And now, if you don't mind, I'll leave you to it.'

'There's no need for that,' the man said. 'I was just giving you a friendly hint, that's all. But a helping hand doesn't come amiss. A helping hand's more use to me than unnecessary advice.'

He looked across at Arnold.

'Nobody at the garage, eh? That's a poor look-out. If something isn't done about it I'll be here all day.'

'Let's get him away,' said Arnold to Peter, 'and be done with him!'

The man got back in the car. They pushed: Arnold in the middle, Peter at one side, Jane at the other. They pushed the car out from the parking-space on to Skirlston Quay. They pushed, first at a walking pace, then at a trot. They were just beginning to

tire when the man let in the clutch, the car jerked, the engine stuttered and fired. In a moment blue smoke was pouring from the exhaust and the car was moving on its own.

Peter, Jane and Arnold slackened pace. The driver didn't stop to thank them, didn't wave. The car drew away towards the road that would take it out of Skirlston; dwindled out of sight and hearing.

'Well!' said Peter. 'So much for that!'

'At least,' said Arnold with feeling, 'he's gone!'

Peter looked at him curiously. Peter was always curious. He liked to know what made people say the things they said and do the things they did. But Arnold didn't tell him anything more. There was a moment's awkward pause. Then:

'I'm Peter Ellison,' Peter said. 'This is Jane.'

Arnold was still silent.

'We just came yesterday,' Peter added. 'We're at the Hendrys'.'

'I know.'

'You live around here, then?'

'Aye. At Cottontree House. The shop.'

Arnold looked steadily at Peter, taking his time over it. Peter was fair. His blue-grey eyes were lively in a narrow, mobile face. He looked back at Arnold with a hint of challenge. Arnold turned the slow gaze on Jane – her face oval, her eyes blue-grey like Peter's, her hair long, straight, a little to the gold side of fair. She smiled faintly as if from a distance, half turned, looked out over the sands.

Then the stuttering of a car engine came back into earshot, grew louder. The shabby black saloon reappeared, drew near, stopped alongside them. Arnold groaned.

The man opened the car window and beckoned. They went across.

'It's you I wanted to speak to,' the man said to Peter. 'You know what? You're a likely lad. Got something about you, you have.'

'Thank you,' said Peter.

'You could do to learn some manners, of course. But never mind that for the moment. I quite like the look of you in spite of it. In fact you might be useful.'

'Oh,' said Peter.

'I'm a businessman. Maybe you wouldn't think it, looking at me. But I am.'

'That's what he said to me last night on the sands,' said Arnold to Peter. Peter said nothing. The man went on:

'You think of a businessman as having a bowler hat and a brief-case and all that, don't you?'

'He said that to me, too,' said Arnold. 'The very same words.'

'What I may have said to you last night on the sands,' the stranger said, 'is neither here nor there. I'm not sure that you haven't lost your chance. Blotted your copybook. We'll see. But for the moment I'm talking to your pal here. What's your name, lad?'

'Peter.'

'Now, Peter, let me tell you, you can't judge folks' business ability from their looks.' The man winked the eye that moved; the other stared blankly. 'Some of them with their bowler hats and rolled umbrellas are no good when it comes to the point. It's ability that counts, not appearance. Don't forget that, Peter. Never forget that.'

'No,' said Peter.

'You're thirteen, you said. It'll be a year or two before you leave school, eh? Still, things take time in the business world. There could be an opening for you when you're ready. I'll remember you. That's a promise. Don't worry. I'll remember you.'

'And who are you?' Peter asked.

'Ah,' said the man. He thought for a moment. 'I haven't a card with me just now. Doesn't matter to you anyway, does it?' He glanced towards Arnold. 'Ask the dark lad,' he suggested to Peter, and wound the window up.

For the second time the battered black car chugged away along the street and up the hill out of Skirlston.

'He'll be back again in a minute, I dare say,' said Peter.

'I hope not!' said Arnold.

'I think he's barmy,' Peter added. And then, after a minute: 'He said to ask you who he is.'

Peter paused expectantly, but Arnold didn't say anything.

'We still don't know who *you* are, either,' Peter said.

'I'm Arnold Haithwaite,' said Arnold, speaking very slowly. And then the words boiled to the surface and came out with a rush:

'And *he* isn't! Whoever he is, he's not Arnold Haithwaite!'

'I don't suppose he would be,' said Peter, puzzled. 'Funny how we keep going on about who people are.'

'It matters,' said Jane, 'who people are.'

It was the first time she had spoken in Arnold's hearing. Her voice was quiet, unaccented, almost as slow as his. He looked at her, but she was gazing out across the bay again.

'We were just going down there,' Peter said. 'These sands are quiet, aren't they? You don't see anyone on them.'

'You want to be careful,' Arnold said.

'What, quicksands?' Peter asked lightly.

'Oh aye, quicksands. And melgraves.'

'What are melgraves?'

'Sort of little quicksands. Where the current and tide's set up a whirlpool and sucked the body out of the sand. And then there's those bracks. Sandbanks along the river channels. They fall in. And then there's the tide. You need to know your tide times, it comes in so quick. There's enough folk been drowned in this bay to fill Irontown Cemetery twice over.'

'That's a cheerful thought,' said Peter. 'Maybe you could show us where it's safe to go. What we really want just now is to find somewhere to swim.'

'It takes years to learn the sands,' Arnold said. 'Years. And even then they keep changing.'

Arnold had been piling it on a bit. He had been remembering how Peter and Jane had given him a few minutes' anxiety the previous evening. Now he relented.

'You'll be all right this morning,' he said. 'The tide's still going out. But stay this side of the river. And if you want to swim, I'd use the Dip. That's the pool the tide leaves, round behind the dunes to the south.'

'And what about you?' Peter asked. 'Do you ever go swimming? Would you feel like coming with us?'

'I can't swim.'

Peter was astonished.

'You've lived here all your life and you can't swim?' he said. 'And you were just telling us how dangerous it is.'

Arnold smiled.

'I can't swim,' he said, 'and the Admiral can't swim, and half the fishermen at Upskirl can't swim. It's not swimming jobs we do around here. The Admiral reckons swimming wouldn't help you in Skirl Bay. If you had to swim for it, you'd be . . .'

'Too late, anyway,' Peter finished. He considered the matter. 'I think the Admiral's wrong, whoever he is,' he pronounced. 'I think you should learn to swim.'

'Perhaps,' said Jane in the slow, clear voice, 'Perhaps we could *teach* you to swim.'

Arnold looked her in the eye, and this time she wasn't looking past him, she was looking straight at him, but from quite a long way away.

'Perhaps you could,' he said. 'Thank you very much. But I don't have much time. I'm going to the Admiral's just now, as a matter of fact.'

'Obviously,' said Peter, 'you have a distinguished circle of acquaintances.'

'What?'

'I mean you have posh friends, don't you?'

'The Admiral's not posh,' Arnold said. 'The Admiral's not posh at all.'

Chapter Five

Arnold climbed the steep path to the Admiral's cottage on Low Fell. The Admiral was at the door before he had time to knock. Arnold saluted. It was the proper thing in Skirlston to salute the Admiral. In theory you could be fined a halfpenny for failing to do so.

The Admiral had nothing to do with the Royal Navy. His appointment came from the Duchy of Furness. There had been Admirals of the Royal and Ducal Port of Skirlston-in-Furness since 1692. The Admiral had power to give directions to the masters of all ships using the port. He had to supervise the ship-chandleries and bring all smugglers to justice and keep order in the taverns. There were no ships now, no sailors, no chandlers, no smugglers. The only tavern was the Hendry Arms, a respectable country hotel. But the Admiral still drew his salary. It was the same as in 1692 – ten pounds a year. There was also a house and small-holding, for which the Admiral paid the usual Duchy rent of a yearly bunch of wild violets.

The job of Admiral had become hereditary. The last six Admirals had all been called Joseph Hardwick. The last three of them had been Sand Pilot, too. This was a more recent appointment, dating from 1752. The salary was only five pounds a year, but the job was more remunerative because the Sand Pilot got tips for leading parties over Skirl Bay.

The present Admiral, Joe Hardwick, was a man of over sixty with a round, red, battered-looking face and thick white hair. There wasn't anything nautical about him. In his younger days he had been a great wrestler, well known at all the Westmorland fairs. But in the last few years he had put on weight. He found it hard to bend sufficiently to look after his vegetable garden. Arnold did most of that for him. He found it hard to stake out his nets for flat-fish. Arnold did most of that for him, too. And the Admiral found the duties of Sand Pilot rather trying these days. He managed all right on the fine days in summer, when tips were plentiful. But in the early and late seasons, when the weather was often bad and the customers few, he tended to fall back on Arnold.

Now the Admiral and Arnold sat side by side on the bench at the cottage door. It had a fine view across the bay. A few feet away from them was the telescope which was part of the Admiral's equipment as Sand Pilot. In clear weather and daylight – and that was when people ventured on to the sands – he'd be likely to see anyone who got into trouble. In the kitchen behind them a score of gallon glass jars bubbled and popped, for the Admiral fermented his own wine from roots and fruits, and drank it copiously. There were some who said that home-brew would be his downfall. But no one had ever seen him stagger.

'Well, young Arnold,' he said now, 'how goes it?'

'Not so bad.'

'Much in the nets today?'

'Thirty-five pounds, about. Len's taken it to Jones's at Irontown. It'll fetch three pounds fifty, I dare say. Fifty pence for Len, that leaves one pound fifty each for us. Could be worse, I suppose.'

'Aye, lad, it could. I remember times when we couldn't get a penny a pound for fluke. Lived on it us-selves and were thankful for it.'

Arnold had heard of those times before, and would hear of them again. Today he had something else on his mind.

'Joe,' he said, 'who am I?'

The Admiral stared.

'Well, of all the daft questions,' he said.

'But I want to know,' Arnold insisted. 'Who am I?'

'You're not Prince Charles,' said the Admiral after some thought. 'Because if you was, you'd be Prince of Wales and Duke of Furness, and you'd be my boss. And you're not my boss, so you can't be. And you're not Elvis Presley, because you can't sing. And you're not Kevin Keegan, because you don't play football. I reckon you'll have to be content with being yourself.'

Arnold wasn't amused.

'That's no answer,' he said. 'I want to know who I am.'

The Admiral looked shrewdly at him.

'What d'you ask *me* for?' he said. 'Why not your dad?'

'Because he won't tell me.'

'Then I reckon he's got his reasons.'

'Maybe. But *I* reckon I've a right to know.'

'Tell him so.'

'I've told him so.'

'Tell him again.'

'I've told him again.'

The Admiral was silent for a minute or two. Arnold stared sullenly across the bay.

'I'm not telling you anything that Ernest Haithwaite won't tell you,' the Admiral said at last. 'But you're worrying about nothing. This is who you are, young Arnold. You're Ernest's lad, so far as it matters to anyone. In five years' time, when you're twenty-one, you'll be Admiral and Sand Pilot, because I'll retire then, and Tom Blackburn the Duchy agent knows all about it and he's said yes already. You'll have the Duchy salary and the tips, and you'll have the Lower Garden and you'll have the nets and you'll have my boat for the salmon. And when Ernest dies you'll have Cottontree House and you'll have the shop. You'll be well away, young Arnold. That's who you are – a lad with all you'll ever want in the world. A lucky one, and that's a fact.'

Arnold was still scowling.

'What's up, lad? Don't you like Skirlston?'

'Oh aye,' said Arnold. It wasn't a question that had much meaning for him. He'd lived in Skirlston all his life. He didn't like or dislike it. He just accepted it.

The Admiral pondered again.

'You'll find a lass to wed you,' he said. 'With all you'll have, you'll find one soon enough, and she'll mind the shop and take in the visitors.'

'I wasn't thinking of getting wed,' said Arnold.

'Maybe you aren't thinking of it now,' said the Admiral, 'but the time will come. And you'll have a lad of your own some day, I don't doubt. And if you was to call him Joseph Hardwick for his first two names it wouldn't come amiss. My own Joe won't come back, you know. Fifteen years it is since he went off to Seattle, building aeroplanes. He'll not see Skirlston again. So you see, you're like a son to me as well, the only one I've got. And then you start asking who you are!'

Arnold didn't say anything.

'What makes you bring this up just now?' the Admiral asked.

'Oh, nothing.'

'If I was you, lad, I'd let well alone.'

'Maybe you would, but you're not me.'

There was a long pause.

'Well, if you feel you must know, and if old Ernest won't tell you, you could try asking Miss Hendry at the manor-house. I reckon she could tell you something if she was so minded.'

'What's it got to do with her?'

'Miss Hendry knows a lot, about a lot of things.'

'Anyway, she wouldn't talk to me.' Arnold spoke crossly. 'I might just as well ask to talk to Prince Charles. Your boss.'

'Now, now,' the Admiral said. 'I'm only trying to help. Don't bite my head off. Here, come inside for a minute and try a drop of my last year's elderberry wine. Lovely stuff it is. You couldn't tell it from Chateauneuf-du-Pape.'

'From *what?*' said Arnold. It was still a fine day, but since he had seen the stranger on the car park he hadn't felt cheerful any more. He had slept badly and he'd been up early and he hadn't got to know what he wanted and he was tired.

'You having me on or something?' he said. 'Can't you even speak English?'

The Admiral could maintain discipline. He stood up and loomed bulkily over Arnold.

'Do as you're told,' he said, very quietly, 'and shut up.'

Arnold shut up.

Chapter Six

Arnold walked down the hill from the Admiral's, and along the quay, and back into Cottontree House. The shop was empty and the old man was dozing in a chair in the back room. Arnold dug him in the ribs.

'I want to find a swimsuit,' he said.

'A what?'

'A swimsuit. A bathing-costume.'

'What's that to do with me?'

'I thought you might know if we had one.'

'Expect me to know everything we've got in this house, don't you?' said Ernest. But he did know, as always, and was proud of his knowledge.

'She bought half a dozen, years ago,' he said. He meant his wife. 'I told her we'd never sell them. No demand. But she'd try anything. There's two left, or maybe three. In Grandpa's chest in the back bedroom, third drawer down, on the left. Full of moth by now, I shouldn't wonder.'

Arnold found the bathing-costumes. There were two, and one of them was somewhere near his size. They were navy blue with shoulder-straps – old-fashioned to the point of being comic, but this was lost on Arnold, who didn't know or care what people were wearing. He put on the costume, and a coat over it, and plimsolls, and set off again along the quay. Round the point towards the south-west was the Dip – a pool in a natural hollow behind the dunes, refreshed each day when the tide was high and never empty when it was low.

Peter and Jane had found themselves a corner out of the wind. The sun was warm if you could do that. Jane was lying face down on a bath towel, reading a magazine. Peter, digging with a piece of wood he had found, was building an elaborate canal system to link a smaller pool with the big one. His shoulders were white, turning slightly pink already.

'You want to watch out,' Arnold said. 'You'll get sunburned in no time.'

'Yessir,' said Peter.

'Come here,' said Jane to her brother without looking up. 'Pass me the beach bag.'

She rubbed cream into Peter's back and shoulders. Arnold, embarrassed, looked another way. Peter resumed his digging. Jane went on reading her magazine. Arnold sat on a stone, drew his coat round him, looked at the water. He felt uneasy. He wasn't used to coming on the beach and doing nothing. He scraped a plimsolled toe in the sand, popped the pods on a piece of seaweed. He looked at the sun to gauge the time. Not midday yet, tide still going out, air a bit drier than yesterday, wind veering and dropping . . .

Folk said Arnold was slow, and in some ways he was. He was slow at reading marks on paper. He was slow at putting thoughts into words. But he was quick enough at reading Skirl Sands, which are far more complex than any alphabet. He knew what to make of a hundred small signs – of patterns and ripples and colours and textures, of the way the weed was washed up, of the speed and sound of the river running between sandbanks. He could read the Skirl Estuary sky. He could judge by what seemed like instinct the combined effects of wind and tide and rainfall.

Jane was looking at him.

'You can't swim,' she said.

'No,' said Arnold.

'You want to learn.'

Arnold nodded.

'Take your coat off, then. You can't swim in that, can you?'

Reluctantly, embarrassed again, Arnold peeled off the coat. He stood, solid and dark-skinned, in the old-fashioned bathing-costume.

'And your shoes,' Jane said. She smiled, a swift fleeting smile like a glint of light on water.

'I've never taught anyone before,' she said.

Peter looked up from his canal system.

'Being taught's more in your line,' he said.

'Never mind that.'

'Specially Latin. Specially by handsome young men.'

'Stop it, Peter. Arnold, come over here.'

Arnold lay face down on the big towel. He moved his arms and legs frogwise as she told him. He felt, and was, clumsy.

'They don't teach them like that nowadays,' said Peter.

'They do at my school.'

'Your school's out of date. Antediluvian. Opened by Mrs Noah in the Flood.'

'If it was, it'd be diluvian, not antediluvian. You ought to learn some Latin, too.'

Arnold didn't know what this was about. He went on stretching and sweeping back his arms, bending and stretching and closing his legs. Peter came across and helped him. Arnold had trouble in getting into step with himself. He felt foolish and at a disadvantage. Peter began to get bored.

'Try him in the water,' he suggested.

'If you can't do it *out* of the water, you can't do it *in* the water,' Jane said. But after five minutes she felt the same as Peter. They made Arnold kneel in the pool with water up to his chest. He leaned forward, swept his arms apart, flopped and spluttered.

Peter found himself giggling, couldn't help it.

'You look like a stranded whale,' he said.

Arnold tried again, flopped and spluttered. Peter giggled again. Arnold wasn't amused. Jane was sorry for him, and splashed water at Peter to teach him a lesson. Peter splashed water at Jane. In a minute they were scuffling in the water, laughing and shouting at each other, forgetting Arnold. Peter at last swam like a dart to the far end of the pool, climbed out and stood thumbing his nose at his sister.

Jane remembered her pupil.

'Try again,' she said. 'There's nothing to it really, it's only timing.'

Arnold stood glumly with water round his ankles.

'I reckon I should have started sooner,' he said.

He didn't see Peter running round the edge of the pool, coming up behind him. Peter soon got silly; it was a failing of his. Now he shoved Arnold from behind and sent him staggering and splashing forward.

Arnold turned, crossly.

'I'll give you a clout in a minute,' he threatened.

Peter shot away along the side of the pool, hoping someone would chase him. As he did so there was a hiss of dislodged loose sand from the dune above. A round stone, a little smaller than a football, rolled down and into the water. Arnold looked up and caught a glimpse of someone moving.

Instinct made him set off in the direction of the movement, climbing up the side of the dune. But he slithered on the fine sand, slipping back two feet in every three. He got to the top in time to see the back of a human figure disappearing over the next dune, farther inland. And when he reached that dune and could see the footpath, it was empty.

Peter had scrambled up behind him and now stood at his side.

'What was it?' he asked. 'Somebody watching us?'

Arnold nodded.

'A Peeping Tom, I suppose,' Peter said.

'Maybe,' said Arnold. Then, slowly, 'I didn't like the look of that rock.'

'The one that rolled down?'

'Yes. What's a stone that size doing on top of a dune?'

Peter was surprised by the question.

'There's plenty of rocks around,' he said. 'I suppose they get all over the place.'

Arnold didn't look satisfied. They stood in silence for a minute. Then came the sound of a stuttering car engine.

'What does that remind you of?' asked Arnold.

'Don't know . . . Yes, I do. The car we were pushing this morning. But it can't be. That chap'll be a hundred miles away by now.'

'I wonder,' said Arnold. They both listened. The engine noise dwindled. But then they heard a change of gear, and a black car came briefly into their line of sight, pulling up the hill and away out of Skirlston.

'Looks a bit like it,' Peter admitted. 'But I wouldn't be sure. Not at this distance.'

'*I'm* sure,' said Arnold. His face was grim.

'Funny sort of character, wasn't he?' said Peter.

'Not so funny,' said Arnold.

They walked back over the dunes. Peter squatted and slid down the last one in a shower of sprayed sand. Arnold followed. Jane was waiting.

'On with the lesson!' Peter exhorted them.

'I don't think I'll bother about swimming just now,' Arnold said.

'You'll soon learn,' said Jane. She thought he was discouraged. She gave him the momentary smile again. It was like a promise of communication, offered and at once deferred.

'He'll try again,' Peter told her. 'I reckon Arnold's a stayer. That's right, isn't it, Arnold?'

'You could say that,' Arnold said. Then, with slow emphasis, 'I don't give anything up easy. *Anything*.'

Peter was curious. He was curious and he was friendly.

'Arnold,' he said, 'why don't you come to tea with us? This afternoon.'

'Who, me?'

'There aren't any other Arnolds about that I've noticed.'

Arnold frowned. He thought Peter cheeky. He felt that if he knew Peter long he'd have to put him in his place. But Jane smiled, a third time, and that decided him.

'Aye,' he said. 'I will.' And, after a pause, 'Thank you.' And, after a longer pause, 'Well, I'd better be getting on with it.'

He knelt in the pool, with water up to the chest of the old-fashioned bathing-costume. He leaned forward with hands extended together. He flopped, spluttered, recovered, leaned forward again, flopped, recovered.

Chapter Seven

'You're *what?*' said Ernest Haithwaite.

'Going to tea at the manor-house.'

'Going barmy, more like,' said Ernest. 'They won't have the likes of you up there.'

'It's not the Hendrys,' Arnold said. 'They've gone. It's the new folk.'

'Them from the Atomic,' said Ernest. 'Times change, no doubt about it. But what have you to do with them from the Atomic?'

'I met them. The lad and lass, I mean. I was on the beach with them this morning.'

'Oh,' said Ernest. He didn't sound too pleased. 'So *that's* where you were. And who looked after the shop all morning, might I ask?'

'You did,' said Arnold, 'and don't start complaining.'

'I might have been run off my feet,' Ernest said.

'You might have been but you weren't. Nobody comes in on Thursdays.'

'And who made the dinner?' Ernest went on. He pointed with some indignation to the opened tomato-soup can, the sliced loaf and piece of cheese. 'Who got all that ready?'

'You needn't have done anything if you hadn't been in such a hurry. I was back in time.'

'And what about this afternoon?' Ernest was aggrieved by now. 'I suppose I'll have to stay in again all afternoon, while you're gadding about.'

'It won't do you any harm. You wouldn't have gone out, anyway.'

'And isn't there a party to cross the sands at half past three?'

'There is. The Admiral'll take them. I've told him I'm not doing it today. It won't hurt *him*, either. Get his weight down a bit.'

'Eh, I don't know,' said Ernest. He sighed heavily. 'Lads aren't what they used to be. I thought you wasn't like some of them, Arnold, but maybe I was wrong.'

He sighed again, sorry for himself.

'I might've known it'd do no good having folks from the Atomic here . . . Oh, well, lad, if you've set your heart on it I don't want to hold you back. I won't stop you.'

'You *can't* stop me,' said Arnold.

Arnold shaved, for the second time in his life, and put the suit on. It was navy blue serge and had once belonged to Joe Hardwick, the Admiral's son who'd gone to Seattle. Arnold had worn the suit for the last Open Day before he left school and for the last few times he'd been to chapel in Irontown. He didn't care that it was out of fashion, but he was conscious that it was tight and un-comfortable. Still, he felt he owed it to the manor-house. He had great difficulty in persuading himself to go to the front door, licked his lips before ringing the bell, and didn't know what to say when little skinny Norma Benson in maid's uniform answered the door, just as she'd have done in the Hendrys' day. He was relieved when Peter came up from behind her, told her not to bother and joined him outside.

'We're only half unpacked,' Peter said.

'Your mother maybe won't be wanting company, then?' Arnold asked.

'Oh, she doesn't mind. She said, "Your friends are always wel-come, and the more you keep them out of my way the more wel-come they'll be." That's the sort of thing she does say. So I'm keeping you out of her way. Here, let me show you the estate. My father says he's a country gent now. John Ellison, Esquire. We lived in a caravan before we came here, you know. At Windbrake, parked on the site. You had to watch your dinner or somebody else might eat it by mistake, we were so squashed. But now we've got wide open spaces. Jane says we can b-r-e-a-t-h-e.' He flung his arms wide, inhaled deeply.

'Where is Jane?'

Peter winked.

'She's having her Latin lesson.'

The thought seemed to amuse him.

'You must have seen the little red MG in the drive,' he said. 'That's Jeremy's.'

'And who's Jeremy?'

'Aha. Who indeed? Jeremy's a very bright young man. Jeremy's going to Oxford next term to read Classics. Jane can't do Latin for nuts. Jeremy's tuting her. He's coming down from Windermere twice a week all this holiday.'

'Oh,' said Arnold.

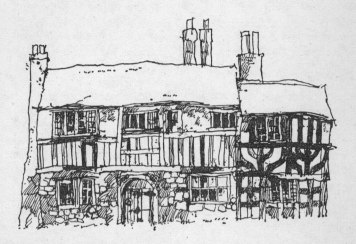

Peter rolled his eyes.

'Oh, Jeremy, Jeremy, wherefore art thou Jeremy?' he said. And then, with a change of tone:

'Actually, Jeremy's a drip ... Now here on our right we have the stables. All they lack is horses.'

Arnold knew about the stables. As a child he had been in the manor grounds many times, unofficially. He could have shown Peter round.

'And this place alongside is where the coachman used to live,' Peter said. 'I'm going to set up my model railway in here. I need shelves all round the sides, to get it at a decent height for working on. Dad'd help me, if he wasn't always tied up at Windbrake.'

'I'll give you a hand myself,' said Arnold, who was good at carpentry. Then he remembered that he had plenty of things to do already for old Ernest and the Admiral and himself. 'If I can,' he added.

'And round the side of the Wing there's a summer-house, and an alleyway under the rhododendrons, and there's a tree with a fork in it that I reckon you could build a cabin in.'

'Oh aye?' said Arnold. He was thinking that Peter was only a lad after all.

They were walking past the Wing when there was a sharp tap on the french window. Peter pulled a face.

'That'll be the old girl,' he said.

'Miss Hendry?'

'That's her. Nice old thing, but dotty. We'll pretend we didn't hear.'

But the rapping on the window was repeated. Peter couldn't help looking round, and having looked round he knew that Miss Hendry knew he had seen her. He wasn't rude enough to walk away after that. Miss Hendry was beckoning now.

'Come on,' Peter said resignedly. Miss Hendry opened the french window for them. They stepped into a big, shabby, chintzy, comfortable room, almost entirely submerged under heaps of papers. On a table stood a typewriter of marvellously antiquated design.

'Hello, Peter,' Miss Hendry said. 'Hello, Arnold.'

Arnold was surprised that Miss Hendry knew him. He knew her, of course. Everyone in Skirlston knew Miss Hendry. She had lived in the manor-house all her life. She drove a Mini around the district, absent-mindedly and with a liking for the crown of the road, but at a speed that gave people ample time to get out of the way. She wrote, when she remembered, a column on country life for *The Cumbrian*. She had been editing, for thirty years, the journals of a sea-captain ancestor, wrecked on his home coast not a dozen miles away. She was chairman or secretary of a dozen organizations. She looked on herself as an efficient businesswoman and committee member. Her manner was crisp. She was scornful of all jokes that were told about eccentric English spinsters, maintaining firmly that in real life such people didn't exist. Nobody would have had the heart, or the nerve, to tell her she was one herself.

Everyone liked Miss Hendry, and feared her a little. Everyone laughed at her – but respectfully, without malice, and strictly behind her back.

'You'll be pleased to know, Peter,' she said, 'that your appointment's been confirmed already.'

'Oh,' said Peter blankly.

'You are now Assistant Secretary.'

Peter seemed taken aback.

'You remember, surely, Peter. Of the Historical Society.'

'Oh yes. Well, you did say something about it, Miss Hendry.'

'I should think I did. It was the first time you came here, long before the removal. You said you'd accept the post. So I put it to the Committee. And they agreed.'

'I – well, I didn't know you really meant it,' said Peter.

'I always mean what I say,' said Miss Hendry severely.

'I don't know whether I'm much good at historical stuff,' Peter said. 'I'm better at maths and electrical things and chemistry and so on.'

'You'll learn,' said Miss Hendry. 'I shall teach you myself. Not that you need do anything very difficult at first. You can write letters and address envelopes.'

Peter's face lengthened.

'It won't be a great deal of work,' Miss Hendry assured him. 'You needn't come to all the meetings. And, I should have said, there's an honorarium.'

'An honorarium? You mean money?'

'Certainly. It's at my discretion. I thought perhaps fifty pence for an afternoon's or evening's help?'

Peter brightened again. It was always useful to earn fifty pence.

'And can I use the typewriter?' he asked.

'Of course you can. If it will let you, that is. It's a shade temperamental, I'm afraid.'

The typewriter did indeed look rather alarming. But Peter was intrigued by all machinery. He went over to it and put in a piece of paper headed:

DUCHY OF FURNESS HISTORICAL SOCIETY
Patron: H.R.H. the Prince of Wales, Duke of Furness
Chairman: Col. T. H. Blackburn, D.S.O.
Secretary: Miss K. E. Hendry, M.A.

Peter added underneath, laboriously:

Assistant Secretary: P. W. H. Ellison

'I don't suppose Prince Charles goes to all the meetings, either,' he said.

'No, I'm afraid not.'

'Oh well, that makes two of us,' said Peter.

Miss Hendry was looking speculatively at Arnold. Instinctively Arnold knew what the look meant. She was thinking of a useful job for him. But Arnold had enough jobs, and wanted to get in first, anyway, with the question that had been coming to the top of his mind at intervals over the last twenty-four hours.

'Miss Hendry,' he said, 'the Admiral . . . You know the Admiral, don't you?'

'Of course I know the Admiral. What a silly thing to ask.'

Arnold felt crushed already. But he went doggedly on.

'The Admiral said you could tell me something. He said you could tell me . . .'

Arnold dropped his voice.

'It's rather private, Miss.'

'Peter!' said Miss Hendry. 'Out! Don't go far, though. Wait on the terrace there.'

Peter went out with a sidelong glance. His parents never gave him orders as decisively as that. He wondered how he was going to get on in his new appointment.

'Now, Arnold.'

'Miss Hendry, I want to know. Well, I mean, I want to know. I want to know who I am.'

Miss Hendry was thoughtful.

'Old Mr Haithwaite won't tell you?' she asked.

'No.'

'And the Admiral won't tell you?'

'No. He said you might.'

'They think I can take all the responsibilities around here,' said Miss Hendry. She paused.

'Sit down, Arnold,' she said.

Another pause followed. Miss Hendry had given instructions to Peter in a rapid, almost staccato manner. Now she slowed down.

'I suppose it must worry you sometimes,' she said.

'Well, not really. Not until just now. I mean, everybody knows me and I've never bothered. I mean, I think of my dad as my dad, even though I know he isn't. If you know what I mean.'

'Yes, I know what you mean. But, Arnold, you must have seen your own birth certificate.'

'Oh aye. The little one. It says "Arnold Haithwaite, Boy", and the date I was born. It doesn't tell me anything I didn't know.'

'You see, Arnold,' said Miss Hendry, talking partly to him and partly to herself, 'people round here think of any kind of irregularity as a disgrace. And what they do with it is bury it. They think that time will grow over it, and after enough years have passed it will all be forgotten. And nine times out of ten they're right, and after a few years it doesn't matter anyway.'

Arnold sorted this out and nodded.

'It wouldn't have mattered to me,' he said. 'It's – oh, just something. It seems daft when I think about it, and it'd seem even dafter if I told you.'

'I might be able to help you find certain facts,' Miss Hendry said after a minute. 'You have a basic right to know about yourself. But you might not be any happier if you did. At this moment, I think I'd need to be convinced that there were good enough reasons to go against the old man's wishes.'

Her voice was speeding up and sharpening. She finished with her original decisiveness, as if she'd made up her mind.

'My advice is to let it alone, Arnold. If I could tell you where you came from, which at the moment I can't, I still wouldn't be telling you who you *are*. That's up to yourself. The only person who can tell you who you really are is *you*.'

'You mean you won't tell me,' said Arnold.

'If that's what you think I mean,' said Miss Hendry, 'all right, that's what I mean. For the present, anyway.' She went to the window.

'Peter!' she called. 'Peter! You can come in now. We've finished.'

'But, my dears,' said Helen Ellison, 'it's nothing to do with me at all.'

'Then why that funny look?' said Peter.

'There was *no* funny look,' his mother said. 'If you fancied you saw a funny look, then that is a fact about you, not a fact about me. You must have been looking for funny looks.'

'He didn't imagine it,' Jane said. 'There was a certain something, all the time Arnold was here.'

'Perhaps you *both* imagined it,' said Helen. 'But it really doesn't matter in the slightest. I didn't say anything and I'm not going to say anything. And now, after that little diversion, perhaps you'll let me unpack my materials. I thought I might make a sketch or two while the light lasts.'

'You looked,' said Peter, 'as if you thought we'd brought home somebody unsuitable.'

'Really, Peter!' said Helen sharply. ' "Unsuitable", indeed! I'm sure you never heard *me* use such a word.'

'I felt it was hanging in the air,' said Peter.

'Then you were mistaken,' Helen said. 'Your friends are your own business. I thought that had been understood for a long time. But since it seems to have arisen, I'd better say I found Arnold perfectly inoffensive. I hope he'll come again. I'm sure we shall get to like each other very well as we know each other better.'

'Well, I expect he *will* come again,' said Peter.

'That's quite all right,' Helen said. 'You've made your point. You've made it without saying it. You want to choose your friends. And I've conceded your point. I conceded it long ago, long before this particular situation arose. It isn't in question at all.'

'Then why are we making all this fuss about it?' Jane asked. 'Why are we calling it a situation?'

'I'm sure I don't know,' said Helen. 'I'm sure I shouldn't have noticed that Arnold wasn't like all your other friends if you

48

hadn't seemed a little *conscious* of it. Normally these things just don't occur to me. I don't attach any importance to them. Of course he does have a slight accent, but these northern accents are perfectly acceptable nowadays.'

John Ellison came in. He had arrived home earlier than usual from the power-station site. John Ellison was a brisk and busy man, and a direct one.

'What's the family conference about?' he asked.

'Don't exaggerate, dear,' Helen said. 'There's nothing so important as a conference going on. We were just having a chat about somebody who came to tea.'

'About Arnold,' said Jane.

'Not the hefty young chap in the tight suit who went down the drive a few minutes ago?'

'That's him,' Peter said.

'We could do with a few like him on the site,' said John Ellison.

Chapter Eight

All through August the Lake District is full of holiday traffic. Some of it spills over to the near-by coast. But not much comes to Skirlston. So far, few tourists are attracted to the desolate Skirl Estuary, with the Irontown blast-furnaces over the hill to the north and miles of rugged fells to the south.

Still, a little traffic is washed up, like seaweed in a remote inlet, even at Skirlston. Most fine days in August there are three or four cars drawn up on the space beside the old custom-house. A few fishing and fell-climbing people come to the Hendry Arms. Children play on the one safe stretch of sand in front of the quay. The mobile grocery sells ice-cream on its daily visit, and a clutch of buckets and spades appears outside Haithwaites' store.

Arnold didn't see much of Peter and Jane after his visit to the manor-house. First they had unseasonable colds, one after the other. Then they went abroad on a three-week holiday. Then the time came when Arnold knew they were back, but he still didn't see them. The village, which knew everyone's business, knew what they were doing. Jane was catching up on her studies, having done poorly in her end-of-term examinations. Jeremy was still coming twice a week to help her, and sometimes she went up to Windermere with him. Peter was spending most of his time with a friend whose father worked with John Ellison at Windbrake. They hadn't dropped Arnold. It was just that he and they didn't come across each other. The swimming lessons seemed to have lapsed.

Arnold had plenty to do. It was the busiest time of year. Parties crossed the sands every day. The shop did more trade, and Ernest Haithwaite was less and less able to cope with it. It dawned slowly on Arnold that the old man was getting feeble.

'I'll be glad when you're wed, lad, and there's someone to look after all this lot,' he'd say, thinking of the shop and the big shabby house. And, on one occasion, 'You can get wed any time from sixteen. You're not too young to start courting.' But Arnold only snorted. There was no girl of his age in Skirlston except little Norma Benson, who worked at the manor and hung around the cinema or snack-bar in Irontown on her night off. And he wasn't thinking of courting, anyway.

There was no doubt, though, that both house and shop got frowsier week by week. Ernest's efforts were diminishing. He found it hard to get down on his knees, and, having done so, to get up. And he was losing interest in what went on. He lived mainly in the past, talked of little except old times on the railway, and retold scraps of anecdote that Arnold had heard a score of times before. He had always been an early riser, but he began to lie in bed in the morning until Arnold scolded him into action. And Arnold, grousing, added some elementary cleaning to his daily activities.

Arnold missed the Ellisons a little when he thought about them. But their absence was more than balanced by that of the man who had claimed his name. As days and weeks went by and he saw no more of the stranger, he grew more and more relieved. After a while he convinced himself that he had seen the last of the other supposed Arnold Haithwaite. He reached the state of half believing he had dreamed it all. The stranger's visit began to seem a faint, puzzling thing of no further importance.

Then the day came when Arnold was hanging nets to dry on the railings at the edge of Skirlston Quay. A prolonged hooting came from behind him. He took no notice at first, but when it didn't stop he looked round to see the man waving vigorously from the window of the old black saloon car.

Arnold turned quickly back to his nets. His heart was racing. He had a wild impulse to leap down the stone steps, to run away across the sands. But that would be daft. He stayed. The stranger drove his car on to the parking-space, left it there at an untidy angle and strode across.

'Now, lad!' he called cordially. He shook Arnold's hand with vigour. 'Told you I'd be back. Glad to see you!'

Arnold scowled.

'Cheer up, young fellow!' the stranger told him. 'It's a bit of business for you. I'll be staying with you again tonight.'

'We're full,' said Arnold. It was a lie, but it came straight to his lips and was out before he had time to think.

'Get away!' the man said. 'That place, full? I'll never believe it. Not till I hear it from the old chap, anyroad. Why, I'd almost think you wanted to get rid of me.'

'You might not be far wrong, at that,' Arnold said.

The stranger didn't take offence. Clearly he was a man of changing moods. Today he was full of bounce.

'You'll have to get to like me,' he said, almost roguishly. 'You'll be seeing plenty of me.'

Arnold scowled again.

'It's a great day, if you did but know it,' the stranger said. 'A great day for me, a great day for Skirlston.'

'Hurray!' Arnold said sardonically.

'I told you I was a businessman, didn't I?'

'You did.'

'Well, it's true. A businessman. A big businessman one day, I don't mind telling you. And you know what I'm going to do?'

Arnold said nothing. The stranger put his face confidentially close. Arnold recoiled a little.

'I'm going to *develop* this town.'

'Oh,' said Arnold. He looked at the stranger's shabby raincoat and beret, and the shabby black car across the road on the parking-space. 'You and who else?'

'Now that's a good question, lad,' the man said. There was a shade of surprise in his voice. 'That's a very good question. I can see you realize there's finance involved in these matters. High finance.'

He fixed Arnold with the one mobile eye. The other eye stared blankly across the bay.

'The answer to "You and who else?" is "Me and my associates". My business associates. I'm expecting to interest a lot of important financiers in this scheme. I'm waiting for replies from them. They'll be competing with each other when they realize what a good thing I'm putting them on to. You know what I'm planning

52

to provide for Skirlston? Something that's all the rage these days. A marina. A centre for pleasure-boating.'

'For pleasure-boating?' Arnold said. 'Where's your water?'

'A bit of dredging, that's all that's needed,' the stranger said.

Arnold was silent. He could have made scathing comments on the hopelessness of Skirl Bay as a place for pleasure-boating – the miles of shallow sands and shifting sandbanks, the constantly changing course of the river, the endless silting, the currents that made the bay perilous in the few daily hours when it had water in it. He could have told the stranger, too, that the man with power over Skirlston was the Ducal Agent, and the Ducal Agent would allow no such scheme even if it were possible. But it didn't seem necessary to say all this. The idea was too absurd for argument. Arnold felt deep relief. His sense of menace faded. A man like this need not be taken seriously.

The stranger took his silence as meaning that he was impressed.

'And that's only the start,' he said. 'You know what else I want to see in Skirlston? A first class restaurant. And a hotel. A twenty-storey hotel. And a shopping plaza. And then when the motor-way comes, with an exit only three miles from here, we'll make a modern resort of it. Britain's leading holiday paradise. Why go to the Bahamas? That's a good line, eh, lad? Why go to the Bahamas when you can go to Skirlston? Glorious Skirlston, 'twixt Lakes and sea. That'll fetch 'em.'

His good eye gleamed. Arnold's spirits rose further. He couldn't think why he had ever let this harmless lunatic alarm him. The struggle on the sands, the attempt to appropriate his name, had just been examples of the man's nonsense – frightening at the time but not worth worrying about now. The stranger went on:

'The main thing with these projects, lad, is to have local opinion on your side. That's vital. That's strategy.' He relished this last word. 'Strategy.'

Arnold was losing interest. He turned back to his nets.

'So I'm developing my local associations,' the man said. 'That's why I've taken the trouble to get to know that old chap of yours. My uncle, I should say. His house is my first foothold here. The modest beginning of my scheme, you might say. My first head-quarters in Skirlston.'

'Oh no!' said Arnold. Dismay rose in him again. 'Not that!'

'Humble it may be,' the stranger said, 'but it's a start. I might even find a place for it in the scheme, just modernized a little, as a bit of old Skirlston among the new. I have a feeling for it, you know. After all, it's family property. Two powerful words, them, "family" and "property". Don't under-rate their importance. Family property, that's what your house is.'

Arnold felt his panic returning, his heartbeat speeding up. He wished he had words to tell this man how wild, ridiculous, impossible his ideas were – words that would send him from Skirlston for ever. He noticed with relief the approach of a familiar figure along the quay.

'It's the Admiral coming,' he said. 'You'd better tell *him* about all this.'

'The Admiral, eh?' said the stranger. He was impressed. 'Fancy that!'

Joe Hardwick drew near. Arnold saluted.

'Admiral,' he said, 'this is Mr . . . er . . .'

He could have kicked himself for a false move. He was inviting the man to take his name again. He dreaded hearing the syllables from the stranger's lips. But, surprisingly, they didn't come. The man appeared not to hear.

'I'm pleased to meet you, Admiral,' he said.

'Folk generally salute the Admiral,' Arnold told him.

The stranger clicked his heels together and saluted smartly. The Admiral approved.

'Well, that was a right salute, anyroad,' he said.

'You really are an Admiral?' the man asked him.

'I am that!' Joe Hardwick said. 'And documents to prove it. Appointed by the Duke of Furness. Which in case you didn't know is Prince Charles.'

'Joe's a special kind of admiral,' Arnold said. 'A local admiral.'

He went on quickly, before the stranger could get a word in:

'This fellow wants to dredge the bay and build a boating centre and a restaurant and a posh hotel and a shopping place and I don't know what else,' he said. 'How do you like that?'

He expected the Admiral to roar with laughter. He had forgotten that Joe Hardwick was a leg-puller. Instead of laughing, he looked at the stranger round-eyed.

'Well, that's a grand idea,' he said seriously. 'The sooner the better, say I. Will we be having it all this year?'

'Nay, it can't be *that* quick,' the stranger said. 'These things take time, you know. If you was used to business you'd realize it. It doesn't do to be in too much of a hurry. But it'll come, I can tell you that. It'll come.'

'If there's anything I can do to help,' said the Admiral, straight-faced, 'you've only to ask. I don't mind digging out a bit of sand myself.'

'Oh, we use mechanized methods these days,' the man said. His tone was patronizing. But he clearly approved much more of the Admiral than of Arnold.

'Don't you have any uniform, Admiral?' he asked.

'Uniform? Joe in uniform?' To Arnold the thought was ludicrous. 'He doesn't have a uniform. What would he want that for? "Admiral's" only a title, you know. He hasn't to *do* anything.'

'He should have a uniform,' said the stranger decisively. 'In fact, Admiral, when my scheme's completed I'll see that you get one. At the company's expense. That's not just generosity, of course. It's business. We'll want to exploit anything picturesque we've got in Skirlston, and an admiral in uniform is picturesque. Very picturesque.'

Joe Hardwick's lips twitched. He was managing with an effort to keep his face straight.

'In fact,' the stranger went on, 'we might even find you a job, if you're free and willing to earn a few pounds a week. Does that interest you?'

'Oh aye,' said Joe. He could hardly get the words out. His face was growing pink with suppressed laughter. 'Oh aye. A few pounds a week would come in handy. What would I have to do for it?'

'Well now, let's see. I thought maybe we'd have an underground car-park below the shopping plaza. You could look after that. It isn't every car-park that has a real admiral as an attendant. With a smart, specially designed uniform you'd be an attraction, quite an attrac . . .'

But Joe could contain himself no longer. He swallowed, spluttered, covered his face with his hands, all to no purpose. He broke
down, helpless with laughter.

'Underground c-c-car-park!' he gasped. 'Blasted out of solid rock,
that's what it'd be. And a marina and a hotel and a shopping
plaza. Arnold, lad, it's the age of miracles!'

He leaned against the railings, laughing and laughing. Arnold
was less amused, but a nervous reaction made him laugh, too. The
stranger was not amused at all. His face grew white, his lips were
pressed together. Slowly his hands began to clench and unclench.
Laughter still rolled from the Admiral.

'You think it's a joke, do you?' the man said. His voice was thin
and sharp and rising. 'You think *I'm* a joke?' The good eye blazed.
'You great oaf! You clot, you clown!'

Suddenly he raised his hand and struck the Admiral with the
flat of it, across the cheek. The sound was like a shot. He swivelled
and lashed out at Arnold. Arnold ducked.

'You'll see!' the man said. 'You'll both see! And *you*' – he was
looking at Arnold – 'you cuckoo-in-the-nest, you'll see first! A
joke, eh? You'll see who and what I am!'

Then he was striding away, along the quay and up the street
towards Cottontree House.

The Admiral straightened up, momentarily sobered by the
blow. He stroked his cheek.

'The ...' he began. 'The little ... He smacked my face! The
nerve! The ... the ...'

Indignation fought in the Admiral with returning laughter.
Laughter won. In a moment he was leaning on the railings again,
his sides shaking.

'An underground car-park under the shopping plaza,' he said.
'Me with a specially designed uniform, selling tickets. I haven't
heard anything so funny for years. And a little fellow like him,
too, in a twenty-year-old Ford. And he smacked my face. He
smacked my face. Eh, Arnold lad, haven't you got *any* sense of
humour? Join me in a good laugh for once, you don't get the
chance all that often.' He was helpless again.

Arnold smiled thinly. But he felt slightly sick, his stomach
churning with anxiety. Joe's laughter didn't reassure him. He

wasn't thinking of whether Skirlston would become a resort. He was sure that it wouldn't, or that if it did this man wouldn't have anything to do with it. He was sure that there wouldn't be a shopping plaza, that the Admiral would never be seen around in fancy dress. And yet he couldn't help feeling that the stranger wasn't as absurd as he seemed. Maybe he was playing a part, maybe he was trying to deceive people, maybe he was trying to deceive himself. Maybe he didn't like to be shown that he was deceiving himself. Certainly he was liable to lose control and might well be dangerous when he did . . .

Arnold's stomach churned again. No, it wasn't the thought of marinas and hotels and restaurants that bothered him. It was the thought of an old man in a grey-stone house. It was the phrase 'family property' and the light in the stranger's good eye as he had used it.

'Oh, shut up, can't you, Joe?' he said to the Admiral, crossly.

Joe Hardwick straightened up, looked him in the eye, almost said something, but couldn't. Clutching at the railings he collapsed into laughter again.

Chapter Nine

Arnold staked his nets at half past seven the next morning. The tide was well out then. At eight he was back in Cottontree House. He lit the ancient gas-stove, put bacon in the frying-pan and turned to find the stranger at his elbow.

' 'Morning, young fellow,' Sonny said.

Arnold grunted.

'No hard feelings, I hope,' the man went on. 'On either side.'

Arnold grunted again.

'I told you I'd be staying the week-end,' the man said. 'I spoke to the old chap, after I'd left you and your pal – the Captain or whatever he calls himself.'

'The Admiral,' Arnold said. 'And he doesn't just call himself that. He *is* that.'

'All right, all right. Well, as I was saying, I spoke to the old chap – my uncle – and he said there was plenty of room. He couldn't understand why you'd said you were full up. Glad to have the custom, he said.' The stranger paused. 'Seems to me,' he went on, 'that you've got something against me, young man. I don't know what it is. But I'm not one to bear malice. As I say, we must learn to get on together. Here, give me that pan, I'll finish the cooking for you.'

'It's all right,' said Arnold shortly. 'I've nowt else to do.'

'I'm used to making meals,' the stranger said. 'A bachelor, you know. Got a home of my own to run. There's not many jobs about the house I can't do.'

'Nor me,' said Arnold.

'This place is in a bit of a state, though, isn't it?' the man said.

'Maybe it is,' said Arnold. He didn't much care. 'It does all right for us.'

'It wouldn't do for me, I can tell you,' the man said. 'If you have property, it's worth maintaining. Takes hundreds off the value of a house if you don't maintain it properly. There's a good deal of work to be done here, inside and out, if you ask me.'

'I'm not asking you,' said Arnold.

'If it was mine,' the stranger said, 'I'd be ashamed to let it get like this.'

'Look here,' Arnold said. 'You go and sit in the visitors' room. I'll bring you your breakfast as soon as it's ready.'

'I'm all right where I am.'

'That's what *you* think,' said Arnold. He was angry. 'I'm telling you to go in the visitors' room. That's your place. The kitchen's mine, and you can keep out of it.'

'Oh, so the kitchen's yours, is it?' the stranger said. His voice took on its sharp edge. 'I don't think it's yours. I reckon it's my uncle's. You've no more right to be here than I have. Less, in fact.'

'Get out of here before I clout you,' said Arnold.

The man faced him squarely. He wasn't as tall as Arnold, or as solid. But he was wiry and muscular, and the difference in age was still to his advantage, though in another two or three years it wouldn't be.

'I wouldn't start any funny business if I was you,' he said.

'Funny business? Who started funny business on the sands? Or on the quay yesterday?'

'You bring it on yourself,' the man said. 'And your pal's as bad. But if you're determined to be awkward, all right then, *be* awkward. I'm not going to argue with you.'

The bacon was cooked. Arnold slapped half of it on a plate and shoved it into the man's hand.

'There you are,' he said. 'Take it and eat it and leave me alone.'

He put porridge in a bowl for the old man, and brewed a pot of tea. Ernest Haithwaite hadn't been getting up for his breakfast lately. Arnold took it to him.

'Here you are,' he said ungraciously. 'And when you've had it you can get up. I'll be out all day.'

Arnold ate his own breakfast and left the house. He spent the morning in the Admiral's garden, digging his resentment of the stranger into the soil. At midday the Admiral called him in.

'Good lad,' he said. 'That patch needed digging over, I don't mind admitting. How I'd manage without you these days I don't know.'

'I did it to please myself,' Arnold said.

'You don't like praise, do you, lad? Anyroad, sit down now and give yourself a rest and talk to me while I do my bit of cooking.'

The Admiral was making an elaborate stew for Sunday dinner, adding herbs and seasonings and half a bottle of last year's wine to his meat and vegetables.

'I know you think I'm daft,' he said, 'messing about like this. But to me it's a hobby. Food and wine fascinate me.'

'Aye, well, you don't keep yourself short of them,' Arnold said.

'And *you're* not short of cheek,' said the Admiral. 'And talking of cheek, I've never seen anything to beat that fellow on the quay yesterday. Slapping my face like that! I still can't believe it. Why, there's special old laws signed by King William that cover the Port of Skirlston. Strictly speaking, I dare say he could be hung for assaulting the Admiral.'

'I only wish he could,' said Arnold gloomily.

The Admiral chuckled afresh at the memory.

'He slapped my face! A skinny little fellow like him! It's a good job for him it wasn't thirty or forty years ago, in my wrestling days. I had a temper then, lad. I'd have picked him up by the scruff of the neck and dropped him off the quay.'

'It's all very well for you to laugh,' said Arnold. 'You haven't got him staying with you.'

'Is he at Cottontree House? Well, well. That should be a bit of free entertainment for you. If he has any more of his bright ideas, don't forget to tell me. Underground car-park, eh? Twenty-storey hotel!'

It crossed Arnold's mind to tell the Admiral of his feelings about the stranger, of the incident on the sands and of the way the man had claimed his name. But he looked at Joe Hardwick's round, red face, still creased with laughter, and gave up the idea at once. The Admiral wouldn't take it seriously for a moment. He'd look on it as adding to the joke.

'There, now, lad, don't look so glum!' said Joe. He dropped a heavy, fatherly hand on Arnold's shoulder. 'Cheer up and get yourself a plate and have some of this stew. You'd not find another stew like this within a hundred miles!'

'I bet I wouldn't!' said Arnold. He ate his share in unappreciative silence.

'I'll take today's party across the bay for you,' he said as he pushed his plate away.

'Nay, this lot are mine,' the Admiral said.

'I'll take them,' Arnold insisted. 'Don't worry, I'll give you the tips. I just feel like getting away from Skirlston today, that's all.'

'I don't know what's come over you lately,' the Admiral said. 'You're not the lad you used to be. Glowering and getting bad-tempered and spoiling the fun of things. If it wasn't that I've known you all these years, I wouldn't want to know you now.'

When the tide had turned, a party could set out across Skirl Sands. Today it was mild, with light cloud and the wind only moderate. There were ten in the party. Arnold stalked ahead of them, saying little. A man who had crossed twice before compared him unfavourably with the Admiral.

'The regular guide's a jolly old chap with a great stock of anecdotes,' he told the others. 'This one's not a patch on him.'

'Besides,' said his wife, 'you never feel quite sure you can trust a youngster of his age, do you? I mean, he can't possibly have the *experience*.'

61

'Oh, he'll be all right. The Duchy wouldn't let him do it if he wasn't reliable. I just wish we could have had the old Admiral, that's all.'

Two of the party stayed at the other side to be picked up by cars. Arnold led the other eight back at a brisk pace. The day grew greyer. The woman who hadn't been sure she could trust him needed help to cross the river channel. Arnold gave her his arm with an ill grace, not even looking at her. No one was sorry to see the last of him. The tips were less than they might have been.

Arnold handed over the money and got back to work in the Admiral's garden. No more digging was needed, but there was weeding to do. There was always weeding.

'Your own garden's more in need of it than mine,' the Admiral said, standing over him with a cup of tea.

'I don't feel like working there today,' Arnold said. And he didn't go home until it was nearly dark.

He saw at once that the kitchen and scullery had been cleaned. The stranger was on his knees, with his shirt-sleeves rolled up, scrubbing the passageway that led from the front door past the shop entrance.

'So,' he said, 'you've seen fit to come back at last. Oh well, maybe I've got more done than I would with you around.'

Arnold stared.

'Who told you to do that?' he demanded.

'Nobody told me. Some of us don't need telling.'

'Where's my dad?'

'Your dad? Oh, you mean my uncle. He's in bed. I told him to take it easy today.'

'Oh, you did? And was it any of your business?'

'I suppose you grudge an old man a bit of a rest,' said the stranger severely.

Arnold pushed past him, not taking any trouble to keep his feet off the newly scrubbed part of the floor, and went up to the old man's room. He found Ernest sitting up, smoking his pipe and reading the Sunday paper.

'A fine one you are,' Arnold said. 'In bed all day.'

'It's thanks to my nephew,' said the old man. 'He's been good to me today, he has that. Brought me an ounce of tobacco, to start with. Then he says to me, "You just take it easy," he says. "You've had a lifetime's hard work," he says, "you're entitled to have somebody else do something for a change." Brought me my dinner, he did, and my tea and all. Treated me like a lord. I've not known anything like it since *she* died, and that's a fact.'

'You're sure he isn't moving in?' Arnold asked. He spoke sarcastically, but his heart thumped at the thought.

'Nay, he's off back to Cobchester in the morning,' the old man said. 'Has to go to work. But he's coming again, he says. And I'll be glad to see him, I can tell you. I'd never have thought my cousin Tom's lad would have turned out so well.'

'Cousin Tom's lad?' said Arnold. He was suspicious. 'That fellow's been talking to you, hasn't he? Telling his tales.'

'Of course he's been talking to me,' said Ernest. 'And a right pleasure it was, too. I'm glad to have a chat now and again. And there's nothing like having your own folk to talk to, when you get to my age.'

'You've got me,' Arnold said.

'And a lot of comfort *you* are these days!' said the old man, crossly.

'You make me sick, getting taken in by him,' said Arnold. 'I'd have thought you'd have more sense.'

He was depressed. He had kept away all day because he couldn't bear the thought of being under the same roof as the stranger. But now it was clear that he had made a mistake. He stumped downstairs.

In the passage the stranger was still scrubbing. When he spoke his voice sounded weary.

'Woman's work, this,' he said. 'And not what a man like me should be doing. Waste of time and talent, that's what it is.'

Arnold said nothing.

'I'll have to make some other arrangement,' the man said.

'You don't need to make *any* arrangements,' said Arnold.

'Things need taking in hand,' said Sonny. 'But I can't do any more for now. And I'll be off early in the morning. And here, in case I don't get a chance to tell you later, just listen to me. If my uncle gets ill or anything, you send for me right away. I've given him the address. Don't hesitate for a moment. I'll be over at once.'

The mobile eye fixed itself on Arnold.

'The family must stick together,' the man added. There was a note of triumph in his voice.

Chapter Ten

Arnold stretched out his hands, finger-tips together. He leaned forward in the water, didn't flop, didn't splutter. He swam. With much thrashing and splashing, he made his way in a graceless breast-stroke across the Dip. He stood up at the far end and smiled to himself, thinking there was no one there. Then there was a round of applause. Peter and Jane, swimsuited, with towels and beach bag, were standing on the dune. They slithered down to him.

'You've been practising!' Peter said.

'Aye.'

'You're very clever, Arnold,' said Jane. 'You didn't take long to learn, did you? You're the best pupil I've ever had.'

'He's the *only* pupil you ever had,' said Peter.

'I've been practising for about a month, on and off,' Arnold said. 'I thought I wasn't going to see you any more.'

'We've been away,' Peter said.

'Not all the time.'

'I'm sorry, Arnold,' said Peter. 'We've both had things to do since we got back. We haven't had a chance to come down here.'

'Your mum didn't like me, did she?' Arnold said.

'Yes, she did.'

'She kept looking at me in a funny way. As if I was something out of the zoo. Well, you needn't think I care. We're what we are in Skirlston, and you can take us or leave us. Folk from outside don't understand, anyway.'

'I don't suppose they do,' said Peter. He was finding Arnold tiresome this morning.

'Arnold,' said Jane, 'Mother likes you perfectly well, and so do we. So shut up, will you?'

Arnold didn't know how to take that. But she was smiling. He grinned reluctantly. Peter laughed out loud.

'Come on,' he said. 'I'll race you to the other end.'

'Don't be daft,' Arnold said. 'You can swim rings round me.'

'I'll swim breast-stroke against you.'

Peter still won by yards. He'd have let Arnold win, but he didn't think Arnold would like it. 'You want to teach your pupil some more strokes,' he said to Jane. Then he and Arnold wrestled in the water, splashing each other. Then they all went running on the sand and throwing the ball. Arnold hadn't thrown a ball around since he was ten and hadn't played on the sands ever.

They threw skiers between each other. Peter was best, both at throwing and catching. Arnold was next, but he often misjudged his timing and distances. Jane was worst, and sometimes she missed the easiest catches. Bounce, bounce, bounce and run. But afterwards they swam again, and Jane swam beautifully. She seemed smoother and more at home in the water than running on the sand.

Arnold felt guilty at first, because old Ernest hadn't wanted to get up and look after the shop, and Arnold had told him he had got to. But it was a clear blue day, the wind no more than a faint breath on face or body, and as they played and swam Arnold felt younger than usual. And the younger he felt the less guilty he felt, as if he was just a lad who couldn't be expected to worry about the old man and the shop.

When Peter tired of swimming, though, and started digging channels in the sand, Arnold felt that this was too young for him altogether, and didn't take part. He swam a little with Jane, not splashing her. Then they came out of the pool and he sat beside her, but a few inches away, because he felt you didn't sit too close to Jane.

'Arnold,' she said after a while, 'you're not happy.'

Peter was digging away, out of earshot.

'No,' said Arnold.

'You were for a little while, a few minutes ago. But now you aren't again.'

'That's right,' said Arnold, surprised.

'Why?'

66

'Oh, nothing.'

'I said, why?' Her voice was quiet, but there was a note of insistence in it. Arnold thought she was inquisitive, and nearly said so. Then he looked in her face and saw that she had dropped her guard and was open to him. And he found he could tell her. He couldn't have told Peter, he hadn't been able to tell the Admiral, there'd have been no point in telling the old man. But he could tell Jane. He could tell her about the stranger.

When he had finished she was quiet for some minutes. The pool was shallower now, draining away towards the distant sea. The tide must be well out, he thought, nearing the turn, and he hadn't staked his nets today.

'If you don't mind,' she said, 'I'd like to tell Peter.'

Peter was digging vigorously, bent over his spade, looking younger than ever.

'I don't mind,' Arnold said. 'If you think there's any point . . . I mean Peter's only a lad.'

'But he's cleverer than I am, you see,' Jane said. 'Much cleverer. I'm not clever, Arnold. I'm not clever at all.'

Arnold left them on the beach, because he and the old man had their midday meal at twelve but the Ellisons didn't eat until one or thereabouts. Mrs Benson was waiting for him at the door of Cottontree House.

'About time somebody came,' she told him. 'Been back three times this morning. Door's still locked.'

Mrs Benson was tall, broad, big-boned, heavy – an alarming woman of downright opinion and fierce temper. How she could be the mother of five small skinny children, from Norma down, was a mystery of genetics. Her husband Jack worked for the rural council and did a lot of overtime. Some said he wasn't sorry to be away from his wife for as many hours a week as possible, but others pointed out that the Bensons needed all the money they could get, and that was true enough. Mostly they got along quietly, but now and again there were great rows that resounded through the village.

'Time we had a proper shop in this village,' she said to Arnold sourly. 'Never been the same, it hasn't, since Ernest's missis died.

Used to sell everything, food and all, before that mobile grocery started coming. Nothing to eat now but 'taters and a bit of stuff in cans, and fish if you've caught any. Can't get half of what you want at the best of times. And now it seems to be always closed . . .'

'I told my dad to open up,' Arnold said. 'Wait here a minute.'

He went through the yard and into the house at the back and opened the shop door from inside. There was a card on the floor to say the traveller from the wholesalers' had called. Arnold remembered that this was his day. He felt cross with the old man.

He served Mrs Benson with all he could find of what she wanted, took her money, counted it carefully and found it correct. Then he went upstairs. On the way, fear brushed him briefly – a sudden fear that Ernest Haithwaite might be dead. But he wasn't. The old man was in bed, propped against the pillows. He had been smoking his pipe, but wasn't now. The pipe lay on its side on a newspaper on top of the blankets. Ernest was just looking blankly at the wall. He didn't turn when Arnold went in.

'Well,' said Arnold, 'what's the matter with you?'

'You know very well,' Ernest said. 'I was sick all day yesterday.'

'You were sick yesterday morning. You're all right now.'

'I don't feel so good, lad.'

'You don't look so bad to me.'

Arnold knew the old man hadn't been too well for weeks. His face was grey now, unhealthy-looking. But Arnold wasn't in a sympathetic mood.

'The traveller's been from Smithsons,' he said. 'And Mrs Benson, complaining.'

'I can't help it, lad. We none of us get any younger. Seventy-nine next, then it'll be eighty. I oughtn't to be working at my age. Sonny told me so. "You oughtn't to be working at your age, Uncle," he said.'

'Oh, him!' said Arnold.

'At least I get some sympathy from him,' said Ernest. 'I get none from you.'

But the sorrier he was for himself, the less Arnold was sorry for him.

'You'd be all right if you kept moving,' he said. 'It's all this lying around that sets you back. You never used to be like this. If you want to know, I don't think there's anything wrong with you.'

'You're hard-hearted, lad,' said the old man. He sighed.

'I'll get the doctor over from Irontown if you like,' Arnold said.

'There's no need for that. I could just do to take it easy a bit, that's all.'

'So could plenty of folks,' said Arnold.

Inwardly he relented. There was a sand crossing again this afternoon. He decided to ask the Admiral to take charge, so that he could stay in the shop and the old man in bed. But he wouldn't tell Ernest just yet. It didn't do to spoil him.

'I'll bring you some dinner,' he said.

'I wondered if I'd get anything,' said Ernest pathetically. 'Sonny made me a lovely stew on Sunday. Haven't had a stew like that for years.'

'It came out of a can.'

'It didn't. He made it himself, special. He told me so.'

'I saw the empty,' Arnold said. 'And anyway, you needn't think I'm going to cook you something special. You'll have to make do with what I can find.'

The old man pulled himself up in bed.

'Bring me a pencil, lad,' he said. 'And some paper.'

'What d'you want those for?'

'Just to make a list of some things we need. And bring me an envelope, too.'

'Why an envelope?'

'To put it in, of course . . . I might write to Smithsons.'

Arnold brought him a stub of pencil, a small hairy notebook, an envelope. When he came up a few minutes later with tomato soup and corned-beef sandwiches, the old man was writing laboriously. He held the pad well away from Arnold. Half an hour afterwards, Arnold opened the kitchen door to see him tip-toeing past, heading from the back porch towards the stairs.

'Where have you been?' he demanded.

'Out.'

'I thought you were supposed to be ill in bed.'

'I just wanted to post a letter.'

69

'You could have given it to me to post.'

'I wanted to post it myself.'

'Who were you writing to, eh?'

'I told you I might write to Smithsons.'

'And you might not. What's going on? What are you keeping secret?'

'It's none of your business,' said the old man. Then he couldn't stop himself smiling in sly triumph.

'Happen you'll find out before long,' he said.

'I know already,' said Arnold. 'I could clout you, old as you are. Get back to bed before I lose my temper.'

Chapter Eleven

The shop bell rang as Arnold was finishing his breakfast. It was Peter. He carried a rolled-up towel and swimsuit.

'Coming to the beach?' he asked.

'Not this morning,' Arnold said. 'It's my dad. He's not so well again. I'll have to stay in the shop.'

'That's three days in a row,' Peter said, disappointed. 'Couldn't the shop look after itself a bit?'

'Not on a Saturday,' said Arnold. 'Not when it's as fine as this, and still August.'

'Well, why don't you teach *me* the shop?' said Peter. 'Then maybe I could look after it some time and let you get out.'

'There's not much to teach,' Arnold said. 'It's mainly a matter of knowing where things are. *He* knows that. I don't always know, myself. I go upstairs and ask him.'

Peter seated himself on the counter.

'All right, never mind for now,' he said. 'I wanted to talk to you, Arnold. That's really what I came for. It doesn't matter whether we talk here or at the pool, so long as no one's listening.'

'Well, there won't be anyone along for a while, probably,' said

Arnold. 'Only old Mrs Crowther comes in early on Saturday. But a fine day like this there'll be visiting cars along by midday. We'll be busy this afternoon. Well, sort of busy. Busier than usual.'

'Jane told me,' Peter said. 'About that fellow coming along and saying he's you.'

Arnold nodded. He was embarrassed. He knew once again that he couldn't have told Peter.

'Where is Jane?' he asked.

'Out of action. A full-day session with Jeremy. She isn't getting on too well with that Latin.'

Arnold said nothing and started tidying some cans on a shelf.

'It seemed silly to me at first,' said Peter. 'I mean, it's such a funny thing to make up. Doesn't old Mr Haithwaite *know* it's all a tale?'

'I'm not sure,' Arnold said. 'He won't talk to me about it. But he seems quite taken with this nephew, so-called.'

'And you're certain, are you, Arnold? Positive? That he's not really a nephew?'

'Yes, I'm sure. He was lying. He was lying all the time. And now he talks about family property and says we'll be seeing a lot more of him.'

'And he wants to make a modern resort out of Skirlston?'

'Oh, *that!*' said Arnold. 'That's a lot of nonsense. It couldn't be done. You should hear what the Admiral says.'

'Still,' said Peter, 'one way and another he's up to something. Something very peculiar.'

The light of interest was in his eyes. Arnold was alarmed.

'Now, don't start making it more than it is,' he said. 'This isn't a detective story, you know. This is Skirlston.'

'And they call it a dull old place where nothing happens,' Peter said.

'That's what they say,' Arnold agreed.

'Well,' said Peter. 'It's obvious, isn't it? We've got to find out who he is. And we've got to find out who you are. It's as simple as that.'

It didn't sound simple to Arnold. He didn't like it. His impulse to find things out had worn off after the first rebuffs. The Admiral had told him who he was in practical terms. He didn't care if he never knew any more, either about himself or the stranger, so long as he could have some peace. He had been hoping that if he didn't tamper with things the stranger would tire, would cease to come, would get interested in something else, would let him get on with his life. He had told Jane because she asked and because he needed to tell someone, not because he wanted anything done. Now he wished he hadn't told her.

'So the first thing we must do . . .' Peter said.

Then there were raised voices, just outside the door. Peter opened it. A woman on the pavement was shouting above the sound of the engine to a man still seated in a car that had just drawn up outside.

'Guest-house?' she was calling. 'What guest-house?'

The car was the shabby black saloon car they had seen before. The man was the stranger. He switched off, got out, went towards the woman wagging his finger. She moved towards him, too. They looked angry, looked as if they were starting an argument. Then in the same moment both of them saw the two boys and stopped, as if a moving picture had been halted. After a second or two they went on, but differently. The man smiled, advanced towards Arnold and Peter, and said cordially:

'This is Arnold that I've told you about. This is his friend, a very bright young fellow. And lads, I want you to meet my fiancée, Miss Binns.'

'Hullo!' said Miss Binns.

At first glance she looked younger than she was, at second glance older. At first glance she looked tough, at second glance vulnerable. Probably she was thirty. Her hair was blonde, almost white, her face a little worn. Her mouth was wide and very red, her smile tentative.

'We've come for our holidays,' the man said.

Arnold stared.

'You can't,' he said. 'My dad's poorly in bed. We can't do with you.'

'We're invited!' the man said triumphantly. He waved a piece of pencilled paper in front of Arnold's eyes. 'My uncle invited us.'

'Invited *you*, you mean,' said Miss Binns. 'It wasn't *my* idea. And you said it was a . . .'

'Shut up!' the man said sharply to her. He didn't even turn aside. Then he went on talking to Arnold.

'An invitation in black and white. Said if we wouldn't mind just looking after him a bit, to give you a break ... Your uncle was thinking of *you*, lad, you see. He has your interests at heart. And it'll bring some money in. That's two rooms, both let for a week. We shall pay the full rate, of course. We insist.'

Arnold looked helplessly at Peter. But for once Peter was at a loss. Neither of them said anything.

'Come on, lads, get moving,' the stranger said. 'Give me a hand with Miss Binns's luggage, then I can park the car. She had better have the front bedroom, being the lady. You can put me in that little place at the back.'

Reluctantly, Arnold took two soft-sided suitcases from the back of the car. Peter took the orange fibre one that the man had had with him before. The stranger got back in his car, drove off to the parking-space beside the old custom-house.

'You'd better come through the shop,' Arnold said to Miss Binns.

He walked ahead of her, a case in each hand, to the front bedroom. Peter followed. Miss Binns sat on the bed, looked around her at the marble washstand, the ornamental gilt-edged ewer and basin, the massive convoluted furniture.

'Blimey!' she said. 'The old curiosity shop.'

'You needn't stay if you don't like it,' Arnold told her.

'Oh, I shall like it.' She smiled. She seemed friendly enough. 'It's funny, that's all, funny. He talked as if it would be different. It's such an old-fashioned little house. And the village ...'

'It's deadly dull in Skirlston,' said Peter.

'It's not all that dull,' Arnold protested. But Peter kicked him sharply on the ankle.

'Dullest place in England,' he said. 'Nothing doing after dark.'

Miss Binns considered this.

'Where *do* people go,' she asked, 'if they want a bit of fun?'

'Well, there's a picture-house in Irontown,' said Peter after some thought. 'They call it the bug-hut. Any film you missed twenty years ago, you might see it there.'

Miss Binns pulled a slight face.

'There's a milk-bar in Irontown, too,' Peter told her. 'Getting a bit dilapidated, though.'

'Oh well,' Miss Binns said. 'I like a bit of peace and quiet myself, for a change.'

'It wouldn't be a change if you were living here,' Peter said. 'It'd be every night. Every week, every month, every year.'

'Living here?' said Miss Binns. 'Me, living here?'

Peter wondered if he'd run ahead too far.

'We thought, seeing you're his fiancée . . .' he said.

'What, marry Sonny and live *here*?' said Miss Binns. She laughed. 'I can just see that happening!'

A wave of relief swept over Arnold. Of course it was ridiculous. People like her and a place like Skirlston didn't mix. She wouldn't come here to live, whatever Sonny might think. She'd save the situation. All would be well.

'You can just see what happening?' The thin voice of the stranger came from behind them. He was back from the parking-space, jingling his car keys.

Miss Binns got up from the bed where she was sitting.

'These lads thought we might be planning to get married and settle here,' she said. 'I don't think it's very likely, do you?'

'Don't you?' said Sonny. 'Don't you?'

'Well, of course not.' She laughed again, but there was a faintly uneasy note to it.

'If women get wed,' said Sonny, 'they generally go where their husbands say.'

'Quite the cave-man, aren't you?' said Miss Binns. She turned to the boys. 'Take no notice of him. He isn't usually like this, he's only joking.'

Peter wondered whether the stranger ever joked, and thought he probably didn't.

'I can't see anything daft about settling here,' the man said.

'Well, I mean, look at it,' said Miss Binns.

'You won't know it, or Skirlston either, by the time I've finished with it.'

The brief wave of relief had been followed in Arnold by a trough of depression. He didn't say anything, but his face grew heavy and sullen.

'Now then, you lads,' the man said. 'You've done your part. You're not needed any more.'

Peter went quickly out. Arnold didn't move for a minute. He felt there were important things still to be said. The man seemed to misunderstand.

'Thanks for bringing them cases up,' he said. He dug in his trouser pocket and brought out a tenpenny piece.

'Keep your money,' said Arnold, and turned on his heel.

Chapter Twelve

Arnold, in the kitchen, heard a cough just behind him and jumped.

'Me and Miss Binns,' said the stranger, 'will have our meals in the visitors' dining-room.'

'Have them where you like,' said Arnold. 'What I want to know is, who's going to cook them?'

'Who usually cooks for your visitors?'

'Sometimes me, sometimes my dad. But we only do bed and breakfast. We don't have folks staying all week.'

'Well, you needn't worry,' the man said. 'Miss Binns will see to the meals. After all, it's a woman's work, isn't it?'

'I thought she was on holiday,' said Arnold.

'A change is as good as a rest, they say. Anyroad, she enjoys cooking. At least, she's always saying she wishes she'd time to do more of it. Well, now she has.'

'All right,' said Arnold. He didn't really like having anybody to share the kitchen, but he'd rather have Miss Binns than Sonny because she didn't give him that uncomfortable, apprehensive feeling.

'Except for my uncle's breakfast,' the man said. 'I shall go on doing that. He specially asked me to.'

'He only has porridge.'

'He likes it the way I make it. Apart from that, you can leave it all to Miss Binns. If you watch your step, I might tell her to cook for you as well. Don't say I never think of you. Be a nice change for you, I reckon, to be cooked for properly, by a woman.'

'Oh, aye,' said Arnold. He wondered how keen Miss Binns really was to spend her holiday cooking. She didn't look the domestic type. 'I'm not in for a lot of meals, anyroad,' he said. 'Not at this time of year.'

He didn't see much of either the stranger or Miss Binns for the next two days. High tide was in the small hours, and he was out at breakfast-time each day to empty his nets. He had his midday dinner with the Admiral and led a party across the sands each afternoon. On Sunday he came in to find Miss Binns on her hands and knees, scrubbing the passageway. On Monday she and the stranger were up in the attic all day, and there were great noises of scene-shifting. They came down at tea-time, very dirty. Miss Binns looked pale beneath the grime, and tired.

'I could do with a bath,' she said. 'And you haven't got one, have you?'

'We have,' Arnold said.

'Oh, I never noticed. Where is it?'

'Here, in the corner of the kitchen.'

It was galvanized iron.

'Oh,' said Miss Binns again.

Arnold took it up to the front bedroom, filled it with hot water and withdrew. Miss Binns came down half an hour later, much revived.

'Let's go out and paint the town red,' she said to Sonny. 'We'll see the film at Irontown and have a snack in that milk-bar.'

But Sonny wouldn't stir.

'I'm quite all right here,' he said.

Next day Miss Binns was on her knees again, cleaning out the kitchen, the dirtiest and most-used room of the house. She looked more tired than before. The old man was sick and stayed in his room and Sonny looked after him, not letting anyone else in.

Wednesday was market-day at Irontown, and it also happened to be the day when Arnold found a hundred and twenty pounds of flounder in his nets – the best catch for weeks. This was worth more than the early trade in the shop, so he left the door locked and went off with Len Crowther in the van to sell it. When Peter called at half past nine it was Miss Binns who let him in. She had a duster wrapped round her head and had been washing down the walls of the visitors' sitting-room.

'Spring-cleaning in August, eh?' said Peter, and then, 'You look all in.'

'I am, love,' said Miss Binns. 'Here, how about a cup of tea?'

She went into the kitchen, made tea, came back with a tray.

Before pouring out she reddened her lips, unwrapped the duster from her head, took off her apron, smoothed her dress.

'Funny kind of holiday this is, isn't it?' she said.

'It is,' said Peter. 'Why do you do it?'

'Oh, he took it into his head.'

Miss Binns seemed to think this sufficient explanation. Peter didn't.

'Do you have to do what he says?'

'Well, no, I suppose not.'

'Then . . .'

Miss Binns didn't answer for two or three minutes. She sipped her tea thoughtfully.

'He's a funny fellow,' she said at last. 'He wanted me to come here. He wouldn't have liked it if I hadn't.'

'Look here, Miss Binns . . .' Peter began.

'You can call me Valerie if you like.'

'Listen, just who is he? He said he was Arnold Haithwaite, the same as my friend. But he's not really that, is he? He can't be.'

'No good asking me,' Miss Binns said.

'But you're engaged to him. You must know who you're engaged to. I mean, when it comes to the wedding day you can't say, "I take this man whose name I don't know to be my lawful wedded husband." I mean, can you?'

Miss Binns made an impatient gesture.

'It won't come to that,' she said. 'I don't know who he is. He calls himself Sonny Smith. I know Smith isn't his real name, but that's all I do know.'

'Sailing under false colours, eh?' said Peter.

'Oh, you do go on, lad,' said Miss Binns. 'Bring yourself down to earth. Look, Sonny's one that doesn't give anything away, can you understand that? He won't tell you where he's been, even if it's only to the corner shop for a newspaper. He'll only tell you what he wants to tell you. And it may be true and it may not.'

'And you haven't been to his house?' Peter asked.

'He doesn't stay anywhere for long. He's lived all over Cob- chester at one time and another. Sometimes it's lodgings, sometimes it's places that don't cost anything, like the attic where he is now. Always on his own. Usually he's Mr Smith, but sometimes it's Jones for a change. Don't look at me like that. It's just the way he is. That's Sonny for you.'

'And you're engaged to him!'

'You don't understand, love,' Miss Binns said. 'He wanted me to be engaged to him, same as he wanted to come here. He wouldn't have liked it if I'd said I wouldn't. And if you get involved with Sonny you think twice before you go against him. Because he can be nasty. He has his points, mind you, but there's no denying it, he can be nasty. And . . . well, *sudden*.'

A voice came from across the passage.

'Val'rie! Val'rie!'

'Here!' Miss Binns said.

'I thought I couldn't hear you working. What you up to?'

'Having a tea-break.'

'Oh.'

The stranger came into the room, saw Peter.

'Well, young man?' he said.

'Good morning,' Peter said. 'How's Mr Haithwaite?'

'My uncle? Not too good, I'm sorry to say. He was sick again this morning.'

The man shook his head.

'Very sad,' he said. 'He's gone downhill quite a bit, even in the time I've known him. Of course, he's old, you know. It catches up with all of us in the end, I suppose.' He sighed. 'It wouldn't astonish me if he turned out to be not long for this world.'

He turned to Miss Binns.

'Well, don't you think it's time you were getting on with that cleaning?' he said. 'If I was paying you by the hour, I wouldn't be getting my money's worth.'

'You're not paying me by the hour,' Miss Binns said. 'Or any other way.'

'All right, that'll do . . . Now, lad, you just come with me a minute. I want to show you something.'

Peter followed the man across to the visitors' sitting-room. On the table was a big sheet of cartridge-paper, and the man had been drawing on it with coloured pencils.

'Plans for my marina,' he said. 'What do you think of *that*, hey?'

Peter looked at the map.

' "Hotel",' he read. ' "Pleasure gardens. Esplanade. Boatyard. The Seven Seas Restaurant ..." Sounds smashing. There's not going to be much of Skirlston left if you ever carry this out, is there?'

'What do you mean, *if*?' the man said. 'The question is *when*, not *if*. Anyroad, there'll be quite a bit left. This house, for instance. I can't be pulling family property down, can I? You see, I've left it standing, right on the edge of the new harbour. Magnificent view it'll have. What do you think of that for a plan?'

Peter looked more closely.

'Well,' he said, 'apart from dredging the estuary and blasting away the solid rock the village stands on, I dare say it'll be quite easy.'

'You want to watch out, lad,' said the stranger seriously, 'or you'll be developing your character in the wrong direction. You know what we call folk that's always finding fault? Knockers, that's what we call them, knockers, because they knock everything. There's plenty of knockers in the property world. I've discovered two or three of them since I took an interest in Skirlston. But it's not the knockers that make the fortunes, lad.'

'Have *you* made a fortune?' Peter asked him, and instantly regretted his cheek. There was a momentary light in the man's eye that made his stomach turn over. But when the stranger spoke, his voice was thin and quiet.

'There's time for that, lad,' he said. 'I don't rush things. One step at once. Establish a firm base, that's how you start, and then you expand from that. This is just the beginning of my plans, the very beginning.'

Chapter Thirteen

Next afternoon the wind got up.

There was nearly always wind at Skirlston. When it was a still day down the coast there would be a light breeze here. A moderate wind in neighbouring places meant a strong one in Skirlston. This one wasn't exceptional, but it blew some autumn into the last days of August. It came in with the tide and carried a little squally rain with it. As it strengthened it bent the crouching trees above Skirlston almost into the ground and drove sheep to shelter in the lee of the drystone walls.

The village itself was unmoved. It had been built to stand against the wind. Skirlston pier and quay and the fifty houses were all of hard local stone. Sea and storm, in the long run, will conquer stone and slate; but the long run extends through many life-times.

Arnold battled his way to the pier, to fix in the stone shelter there the notice saying that sand crossings were cancelled. Not that the task was necessary, for no one in his right mind would have set off through flying sand and rain and spray into the grey void beyond the pier's end.

Back on the quay he bumped almost at once into Peter and Jane, wearing capes and sou'westers, heads down and arms linked.

'Come for a walk!' Peter shouted. It was lip-reading and intuition that told Arnold what he meant, for the wind carried the sound away.

'Don't be daft!' he yelled in reply. 'It'll blow you off your feet.'

'It'll what?'

'BLOW YOU OFF YOUR FEET!' Arnold bellowed.

But it wouldn't. He knew the winds round here. It would take a gale of quite a few more knots than this to make walking on Skirlston Quay dangerous. When Jane put her free arm in his and the pair of them swung round, wheeling Arnold into the wind, he went along readily.

It was daft, of course. You didn't walk in a wind like this for pleasure. Normally Arnold would have fastened the doors and windows and sat in the warm fuggy kitchen with the old man, dozing or listening to the radio or catching up with the local paper. But today Ernest Haithwaite had been sick again and was still in bed, and Sonny was playing with his plans on the visitors'-room table, and Miss Binns, after a brief strike in the morning and some harsh words with Sonny, was getting on with her spring-cleaning. There was no comfort at home just now.

Peter and Jane were enjoying themselves. Jane was excited, her face flushed by the wind. They tried to sing, but the wind pushed the words down their throats, so they gave up, laughing. Then they moved in zigzag, a few paces left, a few paces right, taking Arnold with them. It seemed childish, but after a minute or two the spirit infected him. They tramped in step, the three of them in a row, left and forward, right and forward, laughing.

Where the road ended, south-west of Skirlston, they took the footpath that curved round the hill and brought them back, fifty minutes later, to the other end of the village. Peter turned into the manor-house drive. Arnold prepared to unlink, but they wouldn't let him. They carried him along with them, in through the front door, and all three stood in the inner porch, bedraggled and laughing, taking off streaming waterproofs. Without quite knowing what was happening, Arnold found himself, in a pair of John Ellison's slippers, in the big back sitting-room where Miss Hendry had joined the Ellisons for tea round the open fire.

She and John Ellison – home early from the site took Arnold for granted. Anyone could come, so far as they were concerned. Helen Ellison didn't take him for granted at all, was sensitive all the time to his presence and exact position in the room. She wasn't easy with him. But Arnold, warm indoors after a buffeting from the Skirlston wind, was unexpectedly relaxed and comfortable. When Peter and Jane were called on to make toast, Arnold quietly took over. He had years of experience in toasting bread at open fires without getting it scorched or smoky.

Later Arnold vied with Miss Hendry in telling tales of gale and flood. Some of the tales – passed on by word of mouth and not losing anything in the telling – went back well into the last century. Miss Hendry specialized in local history and was well stocked with stories, but Arnold knew even more because of all the hours he had spent talking to the Admiral. Time went by, and he was asked to supper as well. It was nearly midnight when he got back to Cottontree House. All the lights were out except a dim one in the passageway, and it seemed as though everyone had gone to bed.

The wind was still strong, and Arnold reckoned that it wouldn't blow itself out before morning. He went round the ground floor of the house, checking doors and windows. There was a small, high, awkward window open in the back scullery, and a patch of damp where rain had come in. He climbed on a chair to close it, got down, put the chair away and turned to find Miss Binns facing him.

She was distressed. Her eyes were large, her face without make-up was worn and yet younger-looking. She was fully clothed and the suitcase was in her hand.

'I can't stand it,' she said. 'Him and the wind.'

'The wind's nothing,' said Arnold. 'Nothing to what it is in winter sometimes.'

'It doesn't seem nothing to me. It's all very well closing them windows, but it seems to me you can't keep it out of here. I feel as if it was blowing all round me.'

'That's daft,' Arnold said. 'Maybe there's a bit of draught, that's all.'

She shuddered.

'Sometimes I feel as if it was blowing through me. Inside me, almost. I wish I'd never come here. It's horrible. Listen now, the way it's carrying on out there. It's like a baby, crying and crying and nobody comes.'

'It doesn't sound like that to me,' Arnold said. 'That's just the way it blows through the backyard.'

'And *him*. Since we came here I feel as if I wasn't a person. As if I was just something he was using.'

'I feel worse than that,' said Arnold. 'I feel as if I was just something in the way.'

She half smiled, put the suitcase down.

'And there I was thinking you weren't bothered by him,' she said. 'Well, if you want to know, him and this place between them give me the jimjams. If I stayed here much longer, there wouldn't be any me-ness left in me. Do you know what I mean? ... No, you couldn't.'

'I know just what you mean,' Arnold said.

She half smiled again, seemed a little calmer, moved nearer.

'I'll make you a cup of tea,' he said. Then a gust of wind howled through the backyard again, louder than before. In the distance there was a sound as of something crashing from a roof.

85

Miss Binns shivered. The half smile disappeared as if switched off. She picked up the suitcase.

'I'm going,' she said.

'You can't,' said Arnold. 'Not at this time of night.'

'I can. I've got to.'

'What will *he* say?'

'I don't care what he says, as long as I'm not here to hear it. I'll be miles away by breakfast.'

'You'll be lucky if you're out of Skirlston by breakfast. This isn't Cobchester, you know. You can't just hop on a bus.'

'I'll get away somehow. I tell you I've got to.'

'And what'll happen when he catches you?'

'Anything could happen if he did,' Miss Binns said. She shuddered again. 'But he won't. I won't let him. Not till he's had time to calm down.'

'Are you taking the car?' Arnold asked.

'No. He keeps the key in his purse. Anyway, I can't drive.'

'You'd have to get to Ulladale Junction,' Arnold said. 'Twelve miles.' He considered it for a moment. Then:

'Listen,' he said, 'there's no sense in it. You can't go out in this. You'll be soaked in no time, if you're not blown away. You mustn't . . . I won't let you.'

'It's none of your business.'

'It is my business,' said Arnold. 'I don't want anyone that's been staying with us to come to any harm.'

'I shan't come to harm,' she said. 'Anyway, you can't stop me.'

'I can. And I will.'

Miss Binns darted to the kitchen door, turned and stood with her back to it, challenging Arnold with a look.

'You wouldn't touch a woman,' she said.

Arnold knew he couldn't. It wasn't chivalry, it was shyness.

'All right,' he said. 'Go, if you're daft enough. You might as well go out the front, or you'll fall over something in that yard. And listen, go along to Len Crowther's house, just by the petrol pump. If you can make him hear he might just be willing to take you to the station in the taxi.'

'Thank you,' Miss Binns said.

She marched along the passageway. For a moment the front

door was open, the wind blew in, a bit of loose linoleum lifted. Then she was gone.

Arnold walked slowly up the passage and locked the door behind her. Then he thought for a while and unlocked it, just in case she came back. But he didn't think she would. He went to bed.

Chapter Fourteen

The wind was still strong in the morning, but it was lessening. Arnold hadn't staked his nets the previous day, because it hadn't been fit. There was nothing he could do outside, nothing he had to get up early for. He lay in for an hour beyond his usual time. When he went down to the kitchen the stranger was there already, making the old man's porridge.

'How's Miss Binns?' asked Arnold.

Sonny stirred the pan.

'Oh, she's gone,' he said casually. 'Got fed up with it, I reckon.'

Arnold stared. He was astonished – not that Miss Binns hadn't come back but that the man was taking it so calmly.

He tried to sound innocent.

'When did she go?' he asked.

'Some time last night. Didn't bother to tell me. I'm a bit cross about it, I may say. Women!'

Arnold didn't say anything. After a minute the man went on, 'Of course, it's quiet here. Not like it'll be when it's developed. She isn't used to that. And she's had a fair bit to do in the house. Woman's work is never done, as they say.'

'You're not going after her, then?'

'What, me? No. I've more important things than that to do with my time.'

'I thought she was your fiancée,' Arnold said.

'Well, she was,' said Sonny. 'Whether she is now, I'm not so sure. I'll have to think about it. I might not stand for it, carrying on like that. Anyway, she's done most of the work that needed doing here, that's something. And what's it got to do with you?'

'Oh, nothing,' said Arnold. He was thoughtful.

'Go and get me that salt from the scullery,' the man said.

'It's right there beside you.'

'So it is. Well, go and get me one of them yellow basins.'

Arnold went for a basin. When he came back the stranger was bending over the stove, doing something he couldn't see. But he quickly straightened up.

'Pass it over here,' he said. 'Let's hope my uncle's a bit better today. He's not been at all well lately, lad. I hope you realize that. He's not been well at all.'

'Had we better send for the doctor?' Arnold asked.

'Oh no, no,' the man said. 'No need for that. There's nothing he could do that I can't. I'll give the old chap all the care he needs.'

'You won't always be here,' said Arnold.

'Ah. I'm glad you said that. I've got some news for you, lad. In a few days' time I'll be moving in.'

Arnold felt a sickening thump inside his stomach. Not that he was entirely surprised. The possibility had occurred to him more than once, but he had put it out of his mind.

In self-defence he became aggressive.

'Who says you are?' he demanded.

'Who do you think says I am?'

'My dad, I suppose.'

'You'll have to stop calling him your dad,' the man said. 'He isn't your dad. You know that perfectly well. You were taken in off the doorstep, that's what I think, though he's too kind-hearted to say so. And them that were taken in off the doorstep can be put out on the doorstep. So you better watch what you say and do.'

'You've no right here,' Arnold said sullenly.

'I've every right here,' the man said. 'Blood's thicker than water. That old man ill up there, that you're not worrying about, that old man up there's my uncle, my own flesh and blood. I've a right to look after him. And what's more, a duty. Never let it be said that Arnold Haithwaite didn't know his duty.'

'You're not Arnold Haithwaite. I'm Arnold Haithwaite.'

'You?' The man laughed. 'You ever looked in the mirror? You, Arnold Haithwaite? Haithwaites goes back hundreds of years, and you're not one of them. You're here on sufferance, young man, and if I was you I'd behave myself from now on.'

The mobile eye fixed itself on Arnold severely. The other stared aside.

'Anyway,' the man went on, 'you should be glad to have the responsibility taken off your shoulders. From now on it's me that's going to have the worry of it all. And for how long there's no telling.'

'And when do you reckon you'll be moving in?' Arnold asked him.

'End of next week, maybe. I'm going back to Cobchester tomorrow to give my notice in and start getting my things together. It won't take long ... Stop glowering, lad, can't you? Don't you see, I'm not out for myself? I want to give that poor old man the care he needs, and I want to bring this dead-end place into the twentieth century. I'm the best thing that ever happened to Skirlston, only folk don't know it yet.'

'You're not the best thing that ever happened to *me*,' said Arnold.

'You're selfish, lad, that's what you are,' the man said. 'Time you grew out of it.'

'I don't think you want to do anything for Skirlston,' Arnold said. 'I reckon all this marina stuff's nonsense. But you wouldn't mind having a house and a business for nothing.'

The stranger was angry now.

'I've taken as much as I'm taking from you, lad,' he said. 'It's bad enough having ignorance from some of these big firms. Writing letters one line long to say they're not interested, when they haven't even seen the place. But ignorance from a lad of your age, it's more than I can stand. Now get out of my way and let me take my uncle his porridge.'

'I'll take it,' said Arnold.

'You won't,' the man said. 'I wouldn't trust you. I wouldn't trust you with the smallest thing, considering the mood you're in these days.'

'Do you think I trust *you*?' said Arnold.

Chapter Fifteen

'So she went,' Peter said. 'Too quiet for her, eh? I thought it would be.'

'It wasn't that,' Arnold told him. 'In a way I think she quite liked it. It was him, him and the wind. They got on her nerves.'

'And if he stays he'll get on your nerves, eh?' said Peter.

'He's got on mine already. And there's no "if" about it. He *will* stay. He's decided.'

'And what does your dad say?'

'My dad asked him. Or thinks he did. I'm not sure, nor is he. He isn't well, no doubt about it. Sick most mornings and getting weak.'

'I suppose your dad can ask who he likes to stay in the house,' Peter said.

'I suppose he can,' said Arnold gloomily.

'But what if your dad died?'

Arnold had thought of this already. He shrugged his shoulders helplessly.

'If *he* got the house he'd soon have me out.'

Peter was shocked by Arnold's air of acceptance.

'There's such a thing as the law, you know,' he said.

'Oh, the law,' said Arnold. He had never felt the law had much to do with his life.

'Now listen,' said Peter. 'We've got to be prepared, right? So we've two things to do, and it looks to me as if they're getting urgent. Find out who you are and find out who he is. Shouldn't be too difficult.'

It sounded difficult enough to Arnold.

'You'll have to tackle Miss Hendry again about who you are,' Peter said.

'She wasn't keen to tell me anything,' said Arnold. 'And I'm not sure that I want to know any more. I'm not sure that it matters. And what about *him?*'

'There's only one thing to do about him. Follow him back to where he comes from.'

'He comes from Cobchester. Or so he says. He's going there today.'

'We'll follow him back to Cobchester, then.'

'And how do we do that? Stow away in his car?'

Arnold meant to be sarcastic, but Peter said:

'Yes. At any rate, I will.'

Then they both thought of the stranger's small shabby black saloon car. Nobody could hide inside that.

'There's the boot,' Peter said uncertainly.

'Let's walk across and have a look.'

They walked over to the parking-space beside the custom-house. Sonny's car was still there. Peter tried the handle of the boot and it opened at once. There might just have been room for a boy Peter's size to squash himself into it, doubled up, Arnold wondered. But Peter was quicker. He knew his own mind, and he knew when to change it.

'No go,' he said. 'I'd never get out of there. It doesn't open from the inside. Mind you, I probably wouldn't need to get out. I'd have died of cramp or suffocation. That's if he hadn't found me first ...'

'So much for that, then,' said Arnold. He was disposed to write the whole idea off. But Peter wasn't.

'Suppose he hadn't got the car,' he said. 'How would he get to Cobchester then?'

'He'd get the train at Ulladale Junction,' said Arnold promptly. 'Same as Miss Binns must have done the other night. You can get straight through from there to Cobchester.'

'And how'd he get to Ulladale Junction?'

'Len'd have to take him in the taxi. It'd cost him a pound.'

'Let's hope he hasn't spent up,' said Peter. He winked. 'I don't think he knows much about cars, do you?'

'Well, there can't be much wrong with it,' the stranger said. 'It started all right yesterday.'

Len Crowther lowered the bonnet and shook his head. Len was a thin, dark man of thirty. He was reckoned to be on the make – at any rate with visitors. Locals trusted him, for any business carried out between Skirlston folk was within the family.

'Wouldn't like to say what it might be,' he said. 'I'll have to tow it into the garage and have a proper look.'

'I was hoping you might put it right on the spot.'

'Maybe I could,' said Len, 'if I knew what was wrong.'

'But listen, I've got to get to Cobchester today.'

Len considered the matter.

'Can't even look at it till after dinner,' he said. 'I'm on taxi this morning. A job at Irontown.'

This was Arnold's cue.

'Maybe you could take him to the junction?' he said.

The stranger wasn't too pleased.

'I was reckoning to go in my own car,' he said. 'I don't think much of running a car and paying train and taxi fares. I thought you'd have fixed it in no time.'

'All right,' Len said. 'I'll let you deal with it yourself, then.' He made as if to walk away.

'Nay, hold on,' the stranger said. 'I want to get there today, urgent. Maybe I'd better get the train after all.'

'I don't know that I can go to the junction,' Len said. He pondered. 'Might just fit it in. I'll have to charge you two pounds if I do.'

Arnold blinked. That was twice the going rate.

'I gather you're coming back,' Len went on. 'I'll get your car running while you're away.'

'And how much will *that* cost?'

'No idea,' said Len. 'No idea at all. Depends how long it takes.'

Len had a monopoly in Skirlston and for miles around. The stranger groaned.

'All right,' he said. 'I'm ready when you are.'

Len's taxi was at the other side of the parking-space.

'We'll just get this fish of Arnold's aboard,' Len said.

The wind had dropped and Arnold had been able to stake his nets. He had had a good catch. Three boxes of flounder were waiting to be loaded. Some of the fish were alive and flopping around. They went into the back of the taxi with Arnold. The stranger sat in the front seat beside Len.

'I'll take you to the junction first,' Len said, 'then go on to Irontown.'

The man said nothing as the taxi drew out of Skirlston.

'Had a young lady passenger the other night,' Len said conversationally. 'Quite distressed she was. Wet through and in no end of a state. *She* said she had to get to Cobchester, too.'

The stranger still said nothing.

'I wouldn't entertain it at first,' Len said. 'Called out in the middle of the night to take someone to the junction. And a night like that. But she was so upset I couldn't refuse her.'

He paused. There was silence again.

'I'd a feeling she had something to do with *you*,' Len said to the man.

Silence once more.

'Not that it's any of my business, of course,' said Len.

'No, it isn't, is it?' said the stranger.

No more was said all the way to Ulladale Junction. Sonny reluctantly paid Len his two pounds and disappeared towards the booking office. Arnold got out of the car to stretch his legs. Len followed and dug him in the ribs.

'Well now,' he said, 'what did you do with his rotor-arm?'

'Don't ask *me* where it is,' said Arnold.

'You know summat about it,' said Len. 'A rotor-arm doesn't just walk away. It's generally the owner that takes it out, to prevent anyone from pinching the vehicle. But *he* hasn't got it. He doesn't even know it's missing.'

Len laughed heartily.

'Doesn't know the first thing about cars,' he said. 'I wouldn't be surprised if this turned out to be a forty-pound repair job, would you?'

Arnold was shocked. He thought that was going too far, and said so.

'All right, then,' Len said. 'All right. But I don't know what it is, there's something about that fellow that sets my teeth on edge.'

'You can say that again,' Arnold said. They got back in the taxi. He relaxed a little and smiled for the first time that day. In the rack beside the station building he had just caught sight of Peter's bright-red racing bicycle.

Chapter Sixteen

Peter felt silly. He felt as if he was acting in a bad film. Here he was, prowling the corridor of a train, trailing a man to an unknown destination. Trailing a villain? – well, maybe, in a sense, for he believed there was menace in Arnold's stranger and had sometimes felt it himself. But five minutes ago, watching this ordinary-looking man in the soiled raincoat on the platfom at Ulladale Junction, he had wondered if the whole affair was absurd and childish, blown up to a silly height by his own imagination.

Peter was wearing a suit, a collar and tie, and a borrowed pair of spectacles, and had parted and thickly greased his hair. He felt himself sufficiently disguised, for the stranger had seen him at Skirlston casually dressed, without glasses, and with hair blown all over the place. But his sense of improbable melodrama was increased. Without much provocation he could have collapsed into nervous giggles.

He had noted approximately where the stranger got into the train, and as soon as it was moving he walked along to check the compartment. The man had found a corner seat. He had nothing to read, and was looking blankly out of the window. He turned as Peter went past, but didn't show any sign of recognition.

Peter found himself a place in the next compartment but one. He had nothing to do now for the two and a half hours till the train reached Cobchester. The man was there, unsuspecting, and wasn't going to get away from him. He took out a science magazine, found it hard to read with the glasses on and decided he could safely slip them in his pocket. A middle-aged woman in the seat opposite watched him for a few minutes, then leaned across and tapped him on the knee. Peter, still tense, jumped. The woman said:

'Shouldn't you be wearing those spectacles?'

Peter recovered and smiled.

'Oh no,' he said. 'The oculist told me to wear them as little as possible. That's the modern approach. They make the eye muscles lazy.'

'When I was a girl,' the woman said, 'if you had to wear glasses, they made you wear them all the time.' She spoke disapprovingly, as if it showed that things weren't what they used to be.

Peter returned to his magazine. After a minute the woman tapped him on the knee again, and again he jumped.

'You seem to read quite well without them,' she said.

'Oh yes,' Peter said. 'My eyes are improving all the time, they say.'

'They looked pretty strong glasses to me.'

'Yes, well, I don't really need them as strong as that now.'

'Then perhaps it's time you got another pair.'

Peter didn't like the conversation.

'Excuse me,' he said politely, and left the compartment. He went along the corridor and came back to a different one. For a few minutes he read. Then he began to get uneasy about the man. The train hadn't stopped and there was no reason why Sonny should have moved, and yet Peter kept feeling that he might have done. He got up again, put the glasses on, walked the other way along the corridor, past the man's compartment. Yes, he was still there, still looking blankly out of the window.

Peter looked at his watch. He had been half an hour on the train. Another two hours to go. After the twelve-mile uphill cycle ride from Skirlston he was tired, but he wasn't in the state of mind to relax.

It was an edgy and tedious journey. The train stopped twice, and Peter kept anxious guard in case his quarry got out. Between stations he walked three times along the corridor to reassure himself. He felt conspicuous, and the incident with the woman over the spectacles made it worse. He was sure everyone was watching him. By the time the train reached Peterloo Station at Cobchester he was exhausted. And he had a moment's panic when he nearly lost the man in the confusion of getting out of the station.

Outside was a bus-stop. The man stood at it, leaning against the post. Peter lurked in the shadow a few yards away. Sonny allowed two buses to go past, then got on the third, which was nearly empty. Peter had to follow him on to the bus. It was the trickiest part of the operation. Luckily the bus was a double-decker and the man went upstairs. Peter only needed to go inside and watch for him to come down.

The bus drove through thickly built-up areas of the city. It was climbing slightly uphill all the way. Peter noticed the sign WIGAN ROAD. Then the conductor came round for fares. Peter was at a loss; he didn't know where he was going or where he would get off the bus. But while he was still stammering, the stranger came downstairs, leaned over Peter and handed his fare to the conductor.

'I'm getting off here, too,' Peter said. He paid, hoping desperately that he hadn't attracted Sonny's attention. And it seemed he hadn't. The man set off down a side road without a backward look. Peter followed him, staying as far behind as he could without losing the trail. It was early afternoon now, and there were plenty of people around.

They were walking slightly downhill. Peter made mental notes of the street names, in case he needed to find his way back. Camellia Hill, Hibiscus Street, Canal Street. It was a former slum area, rebuilt now with blocks of civic housing, neat, slabby, bricky, dull. But right at the bottom, across a cindery open space, was a contrast with all the new development. It was a single row of ancient cottages on a canal bank, overlooked by a railway viaduct. The cottages were crumbling and decrepit, with black, staring holes where doors and windows had once been. The man strode across the open space and disappeared into the empty doorway at the end of the row.

Peter stepped into the entrance of an apartment block, from which he could keep the cottages in view. It seemed impossible that anyone could actually live in that derelict row. The only explanation he could think of was that the man had gone to fetch something. But time passed and he didn't come out.

Peter grew tired of waiting in the apartment block entry. He was beginning to feel conspicuous again. And he began to distrust his own concentration, for there was only a small gap between the row of cottages and the railway viaduct, and if he took his eyes off it for a second or two the man might cross that space unseen and disappear behind the supports of the viaduct.

Two hours went by. They seemed endless. Peter's spirits sank. He grew more and more convinced that the man had come out of the cottages and he hadn't seen him. He was hungry. The train he had hoped to catch back to Ulladale would leave Peterloo Station at ten past four. There wasn't another until after six. It was clear already that he would be late home tonight, that he might be alarmingly late. At last, frightened but determined, he walked straight across the open space and approached the gaping doorway of the end cottage.

Chapter Seventeen

'Arnold!' the old man called from upstairs. 'Arnold! Is that you?'

'Coming, Dad!' Arnold shouted, half-way there already. He was back from Irontown with three pounds in his pocket from the sale of the day's catch.

Ernest Haithwaite was sitting up in bed. Arnold hadn't seen him for a few days, because Sonny had insisted on taking charge. He was shocked to see how pale and shrunken the old man looked.

'I could do with summat to eat, lad,' he said.

'Well, that's a change,' said Arnold. 'I thought you weren't eating these days.'

'Aye, that's right. I haven't wanted much. Been sick every day. But today I feel a bit more like it. And I haven't had no breakfast.'

The old man sighed pathetically, sorry for himself.

'Didn't he give you any?' Arnold asked, surprised.

'No. He said he was bringing the car round from the parking-space and he'd make my porridge afterwards.'

'I expect he forgot,' Arnold said. 'He's had trouble with the car, you know. Gone to Cobchester by train instead. Len took him. They only just had time to catch it. It probably slipped his mind that you hadn't had your breakfast.'

'I suppose so,' Ernest said. 'He doesn't make porridge like you do, anyway. Funny-tasting stuff it's been lately.'

'Would you like some now, Dad?' Arnold asked.

'Aye. I reckon I could eat an egg or summat, too.'

'I'll do it right away.'

Arnold went downstairs, made porridge and scrambled some eggs. He took the food up on a tray and sat at the old man's bedside. They ate together. Arnold felt cheered. It was something like a restoration of the old relationship. They didn't say much, but he and the old man were comfortable with each other, and Ernest Haithwaite seemed to grow almost visibly stronger as he ate.

'Well, that's better,' he said at last. 'I been wondering if I could get up one of these days.'

Arnold was all in favour of that. The shop needed looking after. 'I don't think it does you any good staying in bed if you don't have to,' he said.

'It was Sonny thought I ought to be in bed,' the old man said. 'Told me I did too much. He said you wasn't looking after me right.'

'Oh, did he?' said Arnold, nettled.

'Nay, lad, don't take it amiss. I'm not complaining.' The old man put a hand out, touched Arnold's. 'It was all right for a bit, doing nothing. But I haven't felt better for it. Felt worse in fact, since he came.'

'What are you letting him come back for, then?' asked Arnold.

'Well, he wants to.'

'It isn't what *he* wants that matters, is it?'

'He's a funny fellow,' the old man said. 'I don't like to say no to him. I feel as if I don't know what might happen if you crossed him. The way he looks at me sometimes . . .'

Arnold's cheerfulness began to evaporate.

'You don't want to let him get a grip on you,' he said.

'I suppose not. It's hard, you know. It's hard when he's there on the spot. He sort of makes you do things.'

Arnold thought of Miss Binns. What she had said about the stranger had been almost the same. And he had made her come here, made her start the fearful task of cleaning up the neglected old house. 'I feel as if I wasn't a person,' she'd said. 'As if I was just something he was using.' She had only got away by escaping at night, in a storm.

'Let's not have him back,' he said.

'It was better when there was just us,' said the old man.

'Well, then,' said Arnold.

'If we could tell him not to come . . .' the old man began.

'That wouldn't work,' Arnold said. 'He'll come back, there's no doubt about that. We'll have to shut the door in his face, that's all. We'll tell him to go away, we don't want him. He can't stay on against your will.'

But the old man was worried by the thought of turning Sonny away.

'He wouldn't like that,' he said. 'I don't know what he'd do.'

'What *could* he do?'

Ernest Haithwaite shivered.

'He'd do something, I can tell you. He wouldn't stand for it.'

Arnold looked at him keenly. For a while the old man wouldn't meet his eye. When he couldn't avoid it any longer, his glance was quick and uneasy, and then he looked down at the floor, abashed.

Arnold could see there was no resistance in him. When the stranger came again the old man would allow him in, would do as he was told, even if it meant he had to go back to bed and die.

The only hope now was Peter.

Chapter Eighteen

There was nothing in the derelict cottage but dirt, damp, rubbish, a smell of cats. Peter walked round inside it, half frightened and half sickened, not sure that the stranger wouldn't jump out at him from some dark corner. But there was nobody there, no place where anyone could possibly be hiding. From a small room at the back a window looked on to the murky water of the canal, shadowed by the viaduct, with a high blank wall opposite.

Peter shivered. He felt both relief and disappointment. The disappointment, he knew, would last longer than the relief. He had lost Sonny, drawn a blank, wasted his journey. But for the moment relief was uppermost. He looked at his watch. Quarter to four. If he could find his way to the main road and get a bus quickly he might still catch that train from Peterloo Station. He could telephone his mother, tell her he'd be home by bedtime, ring off before she had a chance to demand any explanations...

He was standing in the front room working it out in his mind when he heard a thump from somewhere overhead, followed by footsteps. Then there was a creaking sound. Peter looked up, startled. In a dark corner of the ceiling a crack appeared and widened to a gap two feet wide. There was a trapdoor there and it had opened from above. The end of a ladder appeared, waved in the air for a second or two, then slid down towards the floor.

Peter darted into the little room at the back and saw no more. He heard the sounds of somebody coming down the ladder, then a scraping against the wall, then footsteps going out of the cottage and crunching on the cinders outside. Then silence. After a minute or two Peter went cautiously to the front doorway, glanced round it, saw the man disappear round the corner beyond the farthest apartment block and into the street that led uphill. He was a quarter of a mile away and clearly going somewhere. There should be a few minutes' safety at least.

The ladder the man had used was leaning against the inside wall of the front room. The trapdoor was closed, but now that Peter knew where it was he could see its outline in the cracked and dirty ceiling. With his heart thumping, he adjusted the ladder, went up and pushed the trap from underneath. It opened, and a second later he was through it and standing in the space above.

It was a long, low attic, extending over the tops of the four cottages underneath. The side walls sloped sharply, and only in the middle could a grown person have stood upright. There was a camp-bed with grey Army blankets, there was a stove with its chimney going up through the roof, there was a deal table, there were two or three pieces of battered ugly furniture. This obviously was the stranger's home. Peter remembered Miss Binns's words – 'He's lived in all kinds of funny places; you never know where you'll find him next.'

In each side of the sloping roof was one small, grimy window. Through one window could be seen the canal, the viaduct, the high brick wall, a few warehouses. Through the other could be seen the open space in front of the cottages and the street along which the man had disappeared. There was no sign of him now.

Peter didn't know how much or how little time he had. His aim was to find out who the stranger was. There was remarkably little to go on. The room provided only a person's barest needs. There were no letters about, no photographs, nothing with any individuality. Peter pulled open the few cupboards and drawers. Some were empty, some held old brown-edged newspapers or grubby items of men's clothing. Peter replaced everything as it had been, shut all the doors and sat on the bed, baffled. He was still at a dead end. It wasn't just that there was nothing to give away the man's name or any fact about him. It was rather that there didn't seem anything there that made a person belong. An Army billet, even a railway waiting-room, could hardly have seemed more like a place of transit and less like anybody's home. It made the stranger seem more remote, more elusive, more anonymous even than before.

Peter sat for a minute or two, pondering. Then he remembered the danger of his position. He didn't want Sonny to find him here.

He peered through the window towards the street. At first there was nothing to see. Then a movement, down on the right, caught his eye. The stranger was coming back – but he wasn't striding across the cindery space in front of the cottages, he was sidling along by the supports of the railway viaduct, avoiding the open, as if trying not to be seen.

Peter darted to the trap, lowered it behind him and was down the ladder in seconds. He leaned it against the wall where it had been before, and slipped into the little room at the back. He couldn't go out of the front doorway because he would probably meet the man, or at least be seen by him. He looked at the little window-space that gave directly on to the canal. It might just be possible for somebody as slim as himself to wriggle through there and dive into the canal – but it might not, and to get stuck would be disastrous.

He flattened himself against the inner wall of the back room, alongside the doorway. Seconds passed, but he didn't hear the expected sound of the stranger's boots, coming into the house. The seconds stretched into minutes. Peter stayed where he was. The minutes became a quarter-hour, a half-hour. He had missed that train already, and if he stayed much longer he would miss the next one as well. The cottage must be empty. The man must have gone somewhere else. Or perhaps after all it was a different person he'd seen slinking along beside the viaduct ... Peter took a deep breath and stepped into the cottage's main room, heading for the outer doorway and the sunshine beyond.

The sense of menace sharpened suddenly. There was someone there after all; Peter could feel it. He walked steadily towards the light. The man had been standing back to back with him, with the internal wall between them. He detached himself, came after Peter silently. Peter was aware of the grip about to fall on him from behind. He was trying to break into a sprint as the man's hands grabbed his shoulders.

In the dark, the stranger turned him round. He could hardly see anything. Once again his heart thudded.

'Put that ladder up,' the man said quietly.

Peter didn't move. The grip on his shoulders tightened in warning; tightened till it hurt.

'Let me go, then,' Peter said. He went over to the ladder, placed it against the wall.

'Up,' the man said.

Peter went up the ladder, pushed open the trap, stepped into the attic.

The man followed. As Peter turned, his head appeared above the level of the attic floor. Peter shoved, hard. The ladder rocked; the man half fell, half jumped to the cottage floor below. In a moment he was on his way up again.

'I'll kick you!' Peter yelled. The stranger came on. Peter lashed out with his foot. The man seized it. Peter sat down with a bump on the edge of the trap, almost falling through. In a moment the stranger was beside him. In another moment the trapdoor was closed and they were alone together in the attic.

'I saw you,' the stranger said. 'You thought I hadn't, but I saw you. I saw you on the train, I saw you on the bus, I saw you crossing over to here from Canal Street. I thought I'd give you enough rope to hang yourself. And you've hung yourself. You've been in here, spying on me.'

He clenched and unclenched his fists, two or three times.

'I'm strong,' he said. 'You mightn't think it, but I'm strong, very strong.'

'If you touch me,' said Peter, 'I'll scream blue murder.'

'You could scream for twenty minutes here,' the man said, 'and not a soul would hear you.'

He was silent for a moment, looking at Peter.

'Not,' he added, 'that I'd let you scream for twenty minutes.'

Peter said nothing. He could feel the whiteness of his own cheeks. He was desperately frightened.

'Sit down on that camp-bed,' the man went on. 'Hands on your knees.'

Peter did as he was told. The stranger loomed over him.

'You've come from Skirlston,' he said. 'Did that Arnold put you up to it?'

'No,' said Peter.

'Does anyone know where you are?'

'No.'

Peter was afraid of making things worse for Arnold later on.

But he realized as soon as he'd said it that the reply was a mistake. A strange gleam came into the man's good eye.

'If you were missing,' he said, 'nobody would know where to look.'

'Oh yes they would,' said Peter, as confidently as he could.

'That's not what you said a moment ago.' The man sounded triumphant at having caught Peter out.

'They'd find my bike at Ulladale Junction,' Peter said. 'And anyway, although Arnold didn't put me up to this, I did tell him and Len Crowther I was going to Cobchester. And everybody in Skirlston knows what you look like.'

But the wild gleam was strengthening in the stranger's eye.

'Nobody knows where you are,' he said. 'Nobody would ever find anyone down here. It's the end of the world.'

He clenched and unclenched his fists again.

'Supposing,' he said. 'Supposing your body was weighted and dropped through that window into the canal. Supposing you was just left in a corner here, under all that rubbish. How long do you think it would be before they found you?'

'You're mad,' said Peter. 'Stop. Think.' He was trying to be calm, but he could hear his voice rising. 'They'd catch you. Send you to prison. You'd never build your marina. Your marina!'

The stranger wasn't thinking about his marina. Still opening and closing his fists he took a step forward.

Then there were sounds from below.

Something in the atmosphere changed instantly, as if an invisible pane of glass had shattered. The man sat down heavily on the camp-bed beside Peter.

'What do you mean, lad?' he said. 'Mad? Prison? What sort of words is them?'

Footsteps approached across the floor of the cottage below. The ladder scraped. The trapdoor moved up. Hands, with red fingernails, appeared. Then blonde, almost white, hair. Then the face of Miss Binns.

'Hullo,' she said. 'Hullo, lad. I've seen you before, haven't I? Well, Sonny, how's things?'

She stepped off the ladder, sat on the one kitchen chair, lit a cigarette. Her hands trembled a little. She wasn't as calm as she looked or sounded.

'I hope you weren't going to do anything silly,' she said to the man.

'Silly? Me do anything silly?'

A minute's silence followed. Tension was still in the air, but its nature was changing. Sonny's hands were folded on his lap, his fingers still working. Peter felt the man's concentration moving away from himself.

'Well, if you don't mind, I'll be going,' he said lightly, and stood up.

'Hang on a minute, lad,' Miss Binns said. 'You're from Skirlston. You're Peter, aren't you? Got yourself up differently, that's all. What are you doing here?'

The man spoke, his voice now quite flat and dull.

'He was spying,' he said. 'He came down here spying on me.'

'I only wondered who you were,' Peter said.

Miss Binns laughed, a very small laugh.

'That's Sonny's little secret,' she said.

'The lad should mind his own business,' said Sonny. 'He'll be getting himself into difficulties if he doesn't.'

'He's right, you know,' Miss Binns said to Peter. As confidence returned her voice sharpened. 'Of course he's right. You ought to know better than to go nosing around in other folks' affairs. Didn't your parents ever tell you that?'

Peter said nothing.

'If I was you,' Miss Binns went on, 'I'd get out of here, double quick.'

'And not say anything to anyone,' the man added.

'That's right,' Miss Binns said. 'You haven't been here, Peter. Understand? If anybody ever mentions Gumble's Yard, it doesn't mean a thing to you.'

'The dark lad – that Arnold – knows he came to Cobchester,' said Sonny. 'The dark lad knows he was following me.'

'Never mind,' Miss Binns said. She seemed in command now. 'Peter, I want you to tell Arnold, and anyone else that knows you've been to Cobchester, that you didn't follow Sonny after all, but only looked round the shops. You understand, Peter? It's for your own good.'

'If folks was to get to know,' the man said, 'I couldn't answer for what might happen.' He spoke impersonally, as if it was nothing to do with him.

'Now, on your way!' Miss Binns said. She smiled, seeming quite friendly. 'Back to Skirlston and forget all that's happened today. Not a word to a soul!'

Peter felt apprehensive as he passed in front of the man to the trapdoor and stepped on to the ladder. But Sonny was silent, didn't move. Peter was almost out of the cottage below when he heard the stranger's voice again.

'Why did you go?' he was asking Miss Binns.

'Now, now, Sonny,' she said.

'You walked out on me.' The note was rising again, angry, abrasive. 'What right had you? Why did you go?'

Peter heard no more. He walked across the open space, heading for the street that led uphill to the bus-stop. He didn't know how he kept moving, his legs were so weak.

Chapter Nineteen

'Freedom,' said Helen Ellison, 'includes the freedom to be silent. We acknowledge that, Peter. We shall never press you to tell us what you prefer to keep to yourself. And we don't believe in nagging. If you go off for the day without saying anything, we know you must have some good reason. We know you wouldn't be so thoughtless as to worry us unnecessarily. It's just that it all seems so *odd*.'

'Well, I did ring and tell you I'd be late,' said Peter.

'Yes, you did,' said his mother. 'At seven, when you'd been away for ten hours. Still, I suppose not everyone would even do that. We do appreciate it, Peter. We appreciate any courtesy, however slight. But we can't help *wondering*. We're not inquisitive, Peter, not at all, but we do *wonder*.'

'He's home safe and sound,' said John Ellison. 'That's the main thing.'

'Yes, that's the main thing,' Helen said. 'We must be satisfied with that.'

She still looked hopefully at Peter, but he gave no explanations.

'Jane went out for the day with Jeremy,' Helen said, 'and they told us just where they were going and what they were doing and what time they'd be back. And they *were* back, exactly when they said. I thought that was very considerate.'

Helen looked hopefully at Peter once more, but he still didn't respond. The hopeful look turned to a reproachful one.

'Very well, Peter,' she said at length, 'if nothing is what you prefer to say, then by all means say nothing.'

The matter was dropped. But Peter felt himself to be under a cloud for the next few days. The following morning he replaced the rotor-arm in Sonny's car and went to tell Arnold that his mission had failed.

Arnold took the news well. He'd hoped for the best, but he hadn't really expected anything better.

'So that's that,' he said. 'Next Saturday he'll be here for good. He's written to tell my dad so. My dad doesn't want him, you know. He's realizing now that he was daft to encourage a fellow like that. But he won't resist. He hasn't got it in him any more. He'll never resist.'

Peter wasn't without ideas for long. Peter was quick.

'Then we'll organize some resistance for him,' he said. 'The great thing is not to let Sonny in at all. You'll have to have all the doors locked and bolted, and your dad on hand to tell him through the window to go away. I'll be near, too, and if he tries to force his way in it'll be breaking and entering and I'll bring the policeman from up the street.'

Arnold considered this plan.

'He hasn't said what time he's coming,' he objected.

'Well, he's got to get here from the junction, remember. That means sending for Len. I'll fix it with Len to let us know the moment he sets off for Ulladale. In fact, I'll get Len to stand by when he arrives back here, in case there's trouble. We might get the Admiral here, too. We'll keep the blighter out, Arnold, you'll see. We'll keep the blighter out.'

'I suppose it's worth trying,' said Arnold.

August ended. September came in at Skirlston with two or three wet, chilly, almost windless days. At tea-time on the first Friday the weather changed. The breeze freshened. Patches of vivid rain-washed blue appeared between ragged fast-moving clouds. Glimpses of sunshine grew longer. Arnold, looking out from the doorway of the Admiral's house on the hill, watched as waves of light and shade followed each other over the fells, west to east, from Skirl Head towards the Lake District.

'Tomorrow's the day,' he said.

Behind him in the kitchen the Admiral, shirt-sleeved, was busy washing clothes. He reckoned there would be a few hours of good drying weather on the way. Skirlston had a climate of its own, and the Admiral was never wrong about it.

'Tomorrow's the day,' Arnold said again.

'What day?'

'You never listen to me, do you? What have I been telling you about all week?'

'Oh, that fellow. The marina-maker. Your pal.'

'He's no friend of mine,' said Arnold grimly.

'Eh, lad, if you could see your face,' the Admiral said. He bit his lip, tried to prevent himself from laughing and couldn't. 'I'm sorry, but I just can't take that fellow seriously. All his talk about making Skirlston a modern resort and fitting me out with a fancy uniform. Why don't you look at the funny side of him?'

'I don't find him funny,' said Arnold. 'That's why.'

'You never did have much sense of humour, did you, lad?' the Admiral said.

'Can't you tell what's serious and what isn't?' Arnold said irritably.

'All right, all right, don't get worked up. Anyway, I've told you, I'll join the reception committee tomorrow. You get old Ernest to send him packing, and we'll all be there as witnesses. Mind you, I'm sorry in a way. I reckon we'll lose some free entertainment if that fellow leaves Skirlston. And now, just have a look through the 'scope, lad. See if there's anyone out on the sands. If there is, it's time they came in. An hour to high tide, and enough wind to speed it in a bit.'

Arnold didn't think there would be anyone out, because the weather had cleared too recently. But he swung the telescope slowly in a circle, anti-clockwise. First he looked down to the village, to see if there was anyone just setting out. There was no one. The telescope's round eye rested on the pier, the railings along the quay, the octagonal custom-house, the parking-space where the stranger's car still stood. The mobile grocery van was just arriving for its daily visit. You couldn't see Cottontree House from here. The telescope moved on – up the estuary, over the viaduct where the single track of the old railway ran, then round towards Skirl Head. On the way Arnold picked up the Church in the Sea. There were people there – two people on the sand at the foot of the stone island on which the church stood.

Arnold focused on them. Sunshine found them at the same moment as the telescope. Sunshine was reflected from the straight bright hair of the girl. Jane. Beside her was a tall, slim, equally fair young man. That could only be Jeremy. They clambered up the stones towards the church on top, the young man holding out a helping hand to the girl two or three times. Then they sat side by side on the bench outside the church, where Arnold had sat to eat his sandwiches the day that Peter and Jane and the stranger came to Skirlston.

A lot had happened since then, and Arnold had plenty on his mind now, but without knowing why he found the sight disturbing.

'When you've finished,' the Admiral called, 'you can come in and put the kettle on, and we'll have a cup of tea.'

'In a minute,' Arnold said.

Now Jane and Jeremy were looking at something together – perhaps a magazine. The two fair heads bent forward, side by side. Arnold grimaced unconsciously. Consciously he assessed the situation as Sand Pilot. The two were in no danger. They obviously weren't planning to walk back across the bay, because the sports car he'd seen in the manor-house drive was parked at the landward end of the causeway that joined the church to the mainland. And the tide wouldn't cover the causeway today.

'What about that cup of tea?' called the Admiral.

'I said, in a minute!' Arnold called back.

He moved the telescope on. There was an unwritten rule that it was for safety, not for watching people. He swung it back across the empty sands to Skirlston, was about to leave it and go into the cottage when he saw that something wasn't quite the same. He focused on the car-park down by the custom-house, focused on an oblong patch of dry concrete where the rest of the surface was wet. It was the space where a car had been; Sonny's car. In the past five minutes, while he had been looking out across the bay, the stranger's black saloon had gone.

'I suppose I'll have to do it myself,' said the Admiral. He was still thinking about the kettle and his cup of tea. He spoke loudly. But he was speaking to himself. Arnold had pushed the telescope aside and was lumbering away, through the Admiral's garden and down the hill.

As he neared the quay he met Peter, hurrying the opposite way.

'He's come,' said Peter.

'I know.'

'He's just arrived this minute. A day sooner than he said.'

'How did he get here?'

'Came in on the mobile grocery,' said Peter. 'He must have got a lift from Ulladale to Irontown.'

'And where is he now?'

Arnold clung to a shred of hope that the stranger might still have changed his mind, might merely have collected his car and set off straight back to Cobchester. But Peter shook his head.

'His car's in the main street now,' he said. 'Farther up.'

'You mean . . .'

'Outside Cottontree House. I haven't seen him, but he must be there already. He's beaten us to it, Arnold. He's beaten us to it.'

Arnold swore, and not in any genteel way. Peter raised his eyebrows.

'I'll have him out!' Arnold said thickly. Black anger rose inside him. 'I'll have him out! The liar, the skinny little . . .' Muttering to himself, ignoring Peter, he strode off along the quay, towards the main street and Cottontree House.

Peter followed, caught him up on the doorstep.

'You go on to your own house,' said Arnold.

'I'll come in with you,' Peter said.

'You better not. There's going to be a bust-up.'

'I will.'

But even as he spoke, Peter realized that he couldn't. The panic he had felt in the row of tumbledown cottages on the Cobchester canal bank came over him afresh. He couldn't go again to any place where the stranger was. His legs wouldn't carry him. When Arnold jerked a thumb and said briefly, 'Hop it!', Peter obediently continued along the street. A minute later he felt cowardly. He heard the door close behind Arnold, went back to it and stood there struggling with his fear.

'Dad!' called Arnold.

There was no reply.

Arnold strode along the passageway, threw open the door of the kitchen where he had left the old man an hour or two earlier. The smell of tobacco smoke hung stale on the air. But the room was empty.

'Dad!' shouted Arnold again.

Still no reply. Arnold ran up the stairs, two at a time, and into Ernest Haithwaite's bedroom. The old man, in his shirt, was just climbing into bed. The stranger stood beside him.

'Get out!' Arnold said.

The man took no notice.

'That's better,' he said to Ernest. He tucked the blankets in. 'You just stay there. Anything you need, I'll bring it.'

'Get out!' Arnold said again. He took a step forward.

'Don't do anything silly,' said the old man. His voice quavered.

'I'm looking after you now, aren't I, Uncle?' said Sonny. 'Aren't I, Uncle?'

The old man nodded.

'But you told me . . .' Arnold began.

Ernest Haithwaite couldn't meet his eyes.

'Aye, lad, Sonny's looking after me,' he said. 'He reckons I'll have to stay in bed. Been over-tiring myself, like.'

'Get out!' said Arnold to the stranger for the third time.

At last Sonny spoke to him.

'Listen here, young man,' he said. 'You and me's going to have to come to an understanding.'

'Understanding nothing!' Arnold said, and hit him in the face.

The old man jerked up in bed. 'Stop it, Arnold!' he said. 'For your own good, lad. Stop it.'

The stranger stood still. He raised a hand to his cheek, stroked it thoughtfully. A red patch was appearing on it.

'You don't know the risk you're taking,' he said.

The man was calm today. There was no twisting of his fingers. His voice stayed level and under control.

'Go to your own room,' he said quietly.

For a moment, and for the first time, Arnold felt the force of command, almost hypnotic. He turned, on the point of doing as he was told. But the spell was brief. It snapped. Arnold moved in, grabbed the man round the body, tried to throw him.

Then they were on the floor, struggling. Arnold knew how to wrestle, had practised with the Admiral. But the stranger wouldn't be wrestled with in any way that Arnold knew. He was ruthless. He winded Arnold, kneed him, twisted him excruciatingly backwards with his own arm as pivot. In the fight on the sands the stranger had been out of his element. Now he was in control. He didn't hit Arnold, didn't do anything to make a mark, but in half a minute was on top, was propelling Arnold, on a hand and a knee, out of the room, across the landing, through his own door.

The door slammed behind him. He jumped up, opened it, threw himself at the stranger again. But Sonny had won, had won easily. He took his time, dodged Arnold's grip and in a moment had him sprawling again on the bedroom floor.

'Now behave yourself,' he said, and went back to the old man.

Arnold walked dizzily downstairs, opened the front door and stood there taking great gulps of air. Peter appeared.

'What happened?' he demanded. 'Arnold, are you all right?'

Arnold couldn't answer for a moment. He nodded.

'Let's have a look at you.'

Peter led him along the street. In the cobbled forecourt of the Hendry Arms a bench stood against a wall. Peter studied Arnold with care, then seated him gently on the bench.

'Well, you *look* all right,' he said. 'Nothing to show you've been fighting, except that your clothes are a bit ruffled and dusty.'

Arnold had got his breath back now. He felt better physically, apart from twinges of pain in two or three parts of his body. But his gloom was deep.

'He won,' he said. 'I tried to throw him out, and he threw me out instead.'

'You looked to me to come out under your own steam,' Peter said.

'Aye. Well, he didn't actually throw me out, he threw me into my own room. Told me to behave myself. The . . .'

'You can stay at Cottontree House, then?'

'Oh, I suppose I could stay. But do you think I will? Stay there with *him*? No, it's all up now. I'll get a job. Maybe a job on a farm, where I can live in.'

Peter was shocked.

'You're not giving up like that, Arnold?' he said.

'What else can I do?'

'Stay and see it through.'

'I've told you, I won't.'

'Well . . . Listen, why don't we go and see the policeman?'

'Fred Bateman? What can he do?'

'Well, people can't just move into somebody's house and stay there. It's not the law.'

'I'd be surprised if Fred Bateman could shift that fellow,' Arnold said.

But Peter had got up from the bench, was moving already towards the street.

'It can't do any harm to talk to him,' he said.

The policeman stood by Ernest Haithwaite's bedside.

'So this gentleman is your nephew, Mr Haithwaite?' he said. Normally he'd have called the old man 'Ernest', but this was a formal occasion.

Ernest nodded.

'You could say that,' he said. 'He's my cousin Tom's lad.'

'Tell the fellow to prove it!' Arnold said. But Fred Bateman took no notice.

'And you've invited him into your house to stay with you?'

'Aye,' said Ernest. He didn't sound too certain. After a moment he went on, as if he felt an excuse was called for, 'I'm getting old, you know. Not so strong as I was. I need somebody to look after the house and shop and keep an eye on young Arnold here.'

'And what's all this about a fight?'

The stranger stepped forward. The bruise on his face had come up and was looking quite nasty. There was a big scratch on his hand and forearm, too. Arnold didn't remember making it. It had thickened with dried blood and looked much worse than it was.

'The lad attacked me,' he said.

'Is that right, Mr Haithwaite?' Fred Bateman asked.

The old man nodded, though he didn't look happy about it.

'He's a good lad at heart, Fred,' he said.

'But he hit your nephew. Was anything said or done to provoke him?'

Ernest Haithwaite thought for a while. He looked worried, as if there was something in his mind that he hadn't got words for. Then he said, hesitantly:

'No, nothing.'

'He shouted at me three times to get out,' the stranger said. 'Then he hit me without warning. That's right, isn't it, Uncle?'

'That's right,' said Ernest Haithwaite.

'And you used force to defend yourself?' the policeman asked.

'I used the least force I could,' the stranger said. 'You can see that. Who would you think had won, from looking at us?'

'And the lad hasn't been thrown out?' asked Fred.

'I never said I was,' Arnold interrupted.

'You wait till you're spoken to!' the policeman said. There was no sympathy in his voice.

'Thrown out? Not a bit of it,' the stranger said. 'I've told the lad time and again, there's a home for him here as long as he cares to stay, if only he'll behave himself. I've shown a lot of patience, I can tell you. But he doesn't make it easy, carrying on the way he does.'

'So I see,' said Fred Bateman sternly. 'I thought I knew you for a steady lad, young Arnold. I reckon you're getting too big for your boots.' His tone grew more official still. 'It's my duty to give you a warning. You've committed an unprovoked assault. Causing actual bodily harm, that's the words they use in court. You could be in very serious trouble. I admonish you to be of good behaviour in future, else you may have to answer for your actions before the proper authorities.'

The policeman relaxed his formal manner.

'That means, have a bit of sense and stop acting so daft,' he told Arnold in his normal voice.

'Well, I can't understand it,' said Peter. 'I thought you said the old chap was fed up with him, too.'

'So he told me,' Arnold said.

'Then why didn't he speak up?'

'I don't know.' Arnold thought for a moment, then corrected himself. 'Well, I do know, sort of,' he said. 'He's sapped my dad's will. When he's there, my dad just says what Sonny wants him to say.'

'Sonny can't be there *all* the time,' said Peter. 'You'll have to get the old fellow away on his own, some day when Sonny's not there. Take him to a lawyer and tell the whole story.'

But Arnold's mind didn't work like that.

'We keep away from lawyers, here in Skirlston,' he said. 'Anyway, my dad wouldn't say anything. The longer this goes on, the worse he gets. It's not just that he's under that fellow's thumb. He's scared, that's the truth of the matter. He's scared.'

'And well he may be,' said Peter thoughtfully. 'Listen, Arnold. Sonny's moved in. He wants to take the place over, no doubt about that. He won't be wanting to have you and your dad around for any longer than he can help.'

Arnold said nothing.

'And it's not just your dad that has cause to be scared,' said Peter. 'If I was you, I'd be scared, too.'

Chapter Twenty

'Good morning,' the stranger said. He was standing in the doorway of Arnold's room.

Arnold, in bed, turned his face to the wall.

'I said good morning, lad.'

Arnold took no notice.

The stranger said no more. The room was silent. Arnold could only see the wall and did not know whether the man had gone. Minutes passed. Then, as Peter had done in the empty cottage, Arnold knew the man was still there. He felt the urge to turn over and look. The urge grew on him, became almost a physical pain.

He turned over, sharply.

Sonny still stood in the doorway. He hadn't moved in a quarter of an hour. His eye was on Arnold. Arnold's heart started thumping.

'You're late up,' the man said.

'I've nothing to get up for.'

'Your nets?'

'Oh, them,' said Arnold. 'Why should I bother?'

The stranger took two steps forward. Arnold's heart thumped again. But all Sonny said was:

'A bit of fluke fries up nice.'

'Then you can catch some,' said Arnold.

'It'll sell, too. You could sell it in Irontown market.'

'We were selling fluke in Irontown market before you ever heard of Skirlston,' Arnold said.

'Now listen here,' said the stranger. Arnold's clothes were on a chair by the bed. Sonny shifted them and sat down. His voice, always abrasive, softened to a faint scratch. 'We can get along if we try. Why don't you act sensible? Let's come to an understanding, eh?'

'I'm not interested in any understandings with you,' Arnold said. 'All I want is to see the back of you.'

'You'll not be seeing the back of me. I'm here to stay, and you might as well get used to it. And if you're not interested in understandings, then I'll *tell* you. This is how things are going to be. I'll look after the shop. I'll look after the guests. I'll look after my uncle. You don't have to bother with any of those. All I'm expecting you to do is keep the place clean and look after the fires.'

'Just a servant, eh?' Arnold said.

'Call it what you like. You've got to do something for your keep. That's reasonable, isn't it? *I* think it's reasonable. Very reasonable. And if you was to go on netting fluke, and salmon at the right time, it'd do no harm. And if you was to go on taking parties across the sands you'd have some pocket-money, wouldn't you? But that's up to you. All I'm insisting on is the fires and a bit of cleaning. Apart from that you can go where you like and do what you like.'

'And the less you see of me the better, eh?' Arnold said.

'I didn't say that.'

'Well, *I'm* saying it. The less *I* see of *you* the better. I might look for a job somewhere else. On a farm, maybe, where I could live in.'

The stranger half smiled.

'Now that,' he said, 'that's a good idea. That's the most sensible thing I've heard you say yet.'

The good eye gleamed.

'It might be in your own best interest,' the man said. 'It might save you from all kinds of ... difficulties.'

He got up from the chair.

'I wouldn't stand in your way at all,' he said. 'You're free, lad. Free to go.'

'Now do you take him seriously?' Arnold asked.

The Admiral tilted the gallon glass jar, pouring his wine off the dead yeast at the bottom. You needed a steady hand to get the last drops out of the jar without any dregs. The Admiral's hand was steady.

'Aye, lad,' he said. 'I was wrong. You've caught a Tartar there.'
He pushed the empty jar away.

'I'll teach him a lesson for you if you like,' he said. 'A skinny little fellow like him, throwing his weight about. And he smacked my face. I'll show him!'

'I don't think you could,' Arnold said. 'He's half your age.'

The Admiral was a figure of dignity. His dignity would be gone for ever if he lost a fight with the stranger. He was heavy, slow, short of breath. He was a realist, too. In a matter of seconds he had faced the situation, had admitted (though only to himself) that he couldn't do anything.

'Aye, well, maybe it's not worth bothering with,' he said.

'I was thinking,' said Arnold, 'of getting a job on a farm, living in. And then I thought of something else that might be better.' He looked the Admiral in the eye. 'What about coming in with you?'

The Admiral was startled. At first he said nothing.

'I can work,' Arnold said. 'You know I can work. I can do everything for you that I'd have to do for Sonny, and more. I'll see to the house and the garden and the fishing. And maybe, like you said, when you retire I can be Sand Pilot. And you won't be so young then, but I can look after you. Seeing I'm not being allowed to look after my dad, I might as well look after you.'

The Admiral tasted his wine thoughtfully, spat it into the sink.

'That wine'll be all right in a few months' time,' he said. 'Not fit to drink now, of course.'

He drew cork and airlock from another jar and tilted it gently.

All the time he was thinking about what Arnold had said, and Arnold knew he was. The wine drained out, the yeast stayed solid at the bottom.

'Arnold, lad,' the Admiral said at length, 'you're as much as a son to me, you know that. You're all the son I've got nowadays.' He sighed. 'I'll not see my Joe again. Not unless I fly to Seattle, and where would I get the money to fly to Seattle? He'll never come here.'

'Well, then,' said Arnold.

'If it was just for me,' the Admiral said, 'I'd tell you to move in tomorrow. And a happy day it'd be.'

He paused.

'Well, then,' said Arnold again.

'But,' said the Admiral, 'you'd be daft to move out and leave that fellow in control. Daft, daft, daft. You'd have lost, lad, don't you understand?'

'I reckon I've lost already,' said Arnold.

'Where's your fighting spirit?' said the Admiral. 'I'm surprised at you, giving up so easy. I'd have thought there was more grit in you. Seems to me you're not the lad you used to be.'

'Maybe not,' said Arnold. He pondered, gloomily. 'I don't *feel* like what I used to be. It's him, you know. He does something to folk. Sucks the life out of them, almost. But anyway, it's all very well talking about fighting spirit. What can I *do*, Joe? Tell me what I can do.'

'I can't tell you that,' the Admiral said. 'But you'll get a chance. While there's life there's hope, that's what they say. I reckon you should stick it out.'

'You don't want me,' said Arnold. 'That's the long and short of it. You don't want me.'

For a second time the Admiral sighed.

'It wouldn't do, lad,' he said, 'for you to come over here. You'd not be content, not for a moment. You'd be seeing him every day, living in your house, taking your place. I know you, Arnold, I've known you all your life. You couldn't bear it. If you must go, you'd better move right away and look for that job on a farm. But don't say I don't want you.'

His eye met Arnold's over the top of the glass jar.

'I'm sorry, Joe,' said Arnold after a minute.

'All right, lad. Pass me that plastic spoon,' said the Admiral.

Chapter Twenty-one

Arnold mooched. He mooched around Skirlston for days. He wouldn't speak to anyone and he didn't stake any nets. The Admiral took two parties across the sands, but it was getting towards mid-September and the end of the season. The high tides were due soon, and after that there'd be no more sand crossings.

Arnold had no money, but it didn't bother him. He didn't want to buy anything. There was nowhere to buy anything anyway unless he went into Irontown, and he didn't want to go into Irontown. He took bread and cheese from the pantry, and cans of soup and beans from the shop. He made pots of tea for himself when he felt like it. He ate and drank alone. Sonny and Arnold didn't speak, passed each other in silence when they had to. But Arnold knew that he, not Sonny, was suffering; he thought he saw satisfaction in the man's good eye each time they met. Arnold lit no fires, did no cleaning, never saw the old man, who remained bedridden. Arnold mooched.

He knew he couldn't go on like this, knew he'd have to do something soon. The answer would have to be a farm. Arnold didn't know any of the farmers, but Len Crowther knew them all and would find him a place. In a week of eating, sleeping and mooching, Arnold was shifting the ballast of years inside his mind, getting ready to float himself off. Sonny knew it, and Arnold knew that he knew. Sonny was in, and Arnold was on the way out.

On Sunday evening Arnold seated himself at one end of the Coronation bench on Skirlston Quay. There was somebody at the other end, but he didn't notice. He wasn't noticing people much. Only when the macintoshed figure said, 'Hello, Arnold,' in a small voice just audible, did he realize that it was Jane.

He was more irritated than pleased. Only a few days ago he had been disturbed by the sight of Jane with Jeremy outside the church in the sea. It could even be that he had felt a moment's jealousy. But that was in another world. There wasn't room for jealousy in him now, because he'd shrunk into something very small and inward-looking, concentrated on himself.

'I haven't seen you for a long time,' Jane said.

Arnold didn't answer. He gazed out across the bay. It was dusk and getting towards high tide, and the high tides were getting higher. A tongue of water lapped the loose boulders round the island on which the sea church was built. Behind Skirl Head the sky was red from the blast-furnaces of Irontown.

'I heard about that man moving in,' said Jane. 'I'm sorry, Arnold. It must be horrid for you.'

Arnold didn't want to talk to her, didn't want her sympathy. He nearly got up and went. But inertia held him. He couldn't be bothered, he didn't see why he should move.

'I expect you need cheering up,' Jane said. 'So do I. Perhaps we could cheer each other up.'

'Perhaps we could *what*?' said Arnold.

'Cheer each other up.'

'And what have *you* got to need cheering up about?'

'Well, I suppose not much, really, compared with you. I know that, Arnold, but it only makes me feel worse. I oughtn't just to sympathize with you, I ought to feel sorry for old Mr Haithwaite. I suppose if I was really good I'd even feel sorry for that man. I mean, nobody would *want* to be as awful and twisted as that. He must have a wretched life. But I'm not good, Arnold, I don't really feel sorry for anyone, I'm only sorry for myself.'

Arnold made a sound of disgust but didn't say anything.

'And people are so wrong,' Jane said. 'They think I'm thoughtful and considerate and everything, just like another Jeremy. And I'm not, I'm selfish and I don't care tuppence for anybody but me. And I hate myself. And I'm sorry for myself because I hate myself. And I've no business to unload it all on you, because you've got enough already. And I'm a stinker, you don't have to tell me, I know I'm a stinker, but I'm so stinking sorry for myself I don't even care what a stinker I am.'

'Well!' said Arnold. He was jolted out of his self-absorption. He tried to adjust the impression he had of Jane.

'I thought you were so ... you know, so calm,' he said. 'And lucky. You *are* lucky, aren't you?'

'Oh, yes, I'm lucky. I know I'm lucky.'

'Well, then, what's wrong?'

'Everything's wrong.'

'Such as?'

'Oh, just everything.'

'What kind of everything?'

'It's ... Oh, I don't know. I go back to school next week and I haven't got anywhere with that Latin.'

'Latin!' Arnold repeated the word with contempt. 'If that's all you've got to worry about ...'

'Oh, it's not just that, it's everything and everybody, and it's me most of all.'

'You want to have a bit of sense and calm down,' Arnold said.

'I haven't any sense and I can't calm down.'

'Well, get it off your chest, then.'

'All right, but I'm a stinker for telling you, and I know I am, and I don't care. It's my father, because he's always busy and I never see him and when I do see him he's not really there and he thinks he can just pat me on the cheek like a little girl and he doesn't know I'm a PERSON. And it's my mother, always being so cool and pretending she's never ruffled, and so detached and so reasonable and I can't get within miles of her and if only she'd hit me or hug me or shout at me or do SOMETHING. And it's that boy, Peter, he's a child, he's a hundred years younger than me, playing with trains and telling silly little-boy jokes and thinking he's so clever, and he IS so clever and that makes it worse and I can't stand him.'

'I think your family are all right,' said Arnold.

'Yes, I know they are, but just now I can't stand them. And that drip Jeremy; oh, he's so nice, he's so predictable, I know what he's going to say before he opens his mouth, and so reliable, he never gives my parents a moment's anxiety, I only wish he would. And this place. Nothing happens here, nothing ever did happen here, nothing ever will happen here. And me, I'm the worst of all. If you took all the stinkers in the world and multiplied them by a million and rolled them all into one great big enormous stinker you still woudn't have as big a stinker as I am, and I hate, *hate*, HATE myself.' She finished, breathless: 'And I wish I was a boy!'

'All I wish,' said Arnold slowly, 'is that I had somewhere to be.'

She was contrite.

'I'm sorry, Arnold,' she said. 'I know the things I get worked up about are nothing, compared with real worries, like yours. But I told you I was a stinker, and I am. Anyway, I feel better now. I suppose I've been at home too long. There'll be relief all round when they get me back to school.'

'Boarding-school. Do you like it?'

'It's not as bad as some people say.'

'They haven't got any jobs at your school? Strong lad wanted, and so on?'

'Goodness, they won't employ any strong lads *there*. Be realistic, Arnold . . . But are you really thinking of leaving Skirlston?'

'I am that. There's nothing for me here. Not since *he* came.'

'And is there really no way of getting him to go?'

'You tell me one,' said Arnold.

Jane thought.

'If there *was* a way, Peter would find it before me,' she said. 'But he hasn't.'

'The tide's turned,' said Arnold. Whatever happened, he always watched the tide. It had surrounded the church, all except the causeway. That only happened when tides were high. The highest ones of the year were coming now.

'I like that church,' Jane said. 'It's exciting. Specially when the sea gets right round it. I wish that happened more often, don't you?'

'No.'

Jane returned to the subject of the stranger.

'There's just one thing,' she said. 'The man from the Duchy's coming on Tuesday.'

'The who?'

'The man from the Duchy of Furness. The agent. He's an old friend of Miss Hendry's. He's coming to dinner with her. Now if Peter or I could get to see him . . . Well, you never know. I can't help feeling that if somebody spoke quietly to Sonny – somebody important, like the Ducal Agent, that he'd just have to listen to – he might be persuaded to go of his own accord. I mean, he can't really fit into Skirlston permanently, any more than I could, or anyone else that isn't born to it. Perhaps he could be made to realize that he doesn't belong. It would be better for him to see reason than just be thrown out, wouldn't it?'

'Any way of getting rid of him'll do for me,' said Arnold.

'Of course, if he won't listen to reason,' Jane said, 'the Duchy might be able to *make* him leave. The Duchy's all-powerful in these parts, isn't it?'

'I've never had much to do with it,' said Arnold.

'You don't sound very interested in the idea.'

'What do you want me to do, jump for joy?'

'Well, a chance is a chance. It's worth trying.'

'Sonny won't go of his own accord,' said Arnold. 'And the Duchy won't do anything. Nobody'll do anything. And I'm sick of the whole business.'

There was silence for a moment.

'I seem to have cheered myself up a bit,' said Jane, 'but I haven't done *you* much good. And you need it more. I'm sorry, Arnold.'

Over their heads a street-lamp came on. In its hard light Jane's face was a ghostly whitish-grey. But it was open to him. She smiled. There was contact to be made, contact needed. Arnold felt himself starting, painfully, to smile in return. Then the shutter came down in his mind. He was on his own. Sonny had beaten him and he must go.

'I don't know why you're bothering,' he said. 'It's nothing to do with you. And you can't do any good. We're just wasting time.'

Chapter Twenty-two

'I felt rotten,' Jane said. 'And for good reason. You wouldn't understand.'

'I do understand,' Peter said.

'You don't. You might think you do, but you couldn't.'

'Oh yes, I do,' said Peter. 'It's perfectly normal in girls of your age.'

'There should be a society for suppressing precocious small boys,' said Jane. 'Anyway, today I feel better, as if I was twice as light. And yesterday I hated everybody, and today I like everybody again, except myself. I still don't like myself much. I was rather beastly to Arnold. He was so depressed, and I only made him worse.'

'Oh, Arnold . . .' said Peter.

'Poor boy, he's in such a state about that dreadful man. Can't anybody do anything to help?'

'I spoke to Dad. Told him all about it. He says the same as everybody else. He says that whether or not this fellow really is old Mr Haithwaite's nephew doesn't matter terribly, because Mr Haithwaite can ask whoever he likes to stay with him, and Arnold might as well face facts. And I said that wasn't all of it, and that now Sonny's in he'll want Arnold and Mr Haithwaite out. But Dad just thought I was making it into a melodrama. He shrugged his shoulders, the way he does, and said it was time he was getting back to the site.'

'Father doesn't know everything,' said Jane, 'though I used to think he did.'

'Anyway,' Peter said, 'I don't really think Arnold wants to be helped. I passed him in the street the other day and he wouldn't even look at me. I don't see why I should bother. Or why you should.'

'Because I was so foul, that's why I should. If nothing else.'

'To tell you the truth,' said Peter, 'I'm a bit fed up with Arnold. I wish he wasn't here, or we weren't here, or something.'

'We'll both be at school next week.'

'You don't have to tell me that. But it doesn't cure it. He'll still be on our minds. On mine, at least.'

'And mine.'

'I wish I could get him off it,' Peter said, 'and be done with him.'

'The Duchy Agent,' said Jane. 'Mr Blackburn. When he comes to see Miss Hendry tomorrow night, we must tell him – or rather, *you* must, because you're Miss Hendry's buddy. And if he can't do anything, that's it.'

'What if he won't even listen? Like Dad, but more so?'

'You'd better soften up Miss Hendry first. Get *her* interested, and she'll put some pressure on Mr Blackburn, maybe.'

'I'll try,' said Peter.

'Good morning, Mr Assistant Secretary,' Miss Hendry said. She looked at Peter round the side of a stack of papers. 'You've come to catch up with some of that paperwork, I suppose.'

'Well, er . . . yes,' said Peter.

'It's getting terribly behind,' said Miss Hendry. 'I addressed the last lot of envelopes myself.' She looked severe. But somewhere behind the severity a smile was lurking, as Peter knew. He grinned shamefacedly.

'All right,' Miss Hendry said. 'Boys have more important things to do than address envelopes, I know. Now tell me what you've really come about.'

'It's about Arnold. Arnold Haithwaite.'

Miss Hendry tapped her teeth with her pencil.

'I've been expecting Arnold to come and see me,' she said.

'You know about . . . this man?'

'Of course.'

'Well, what are we going to do?'

'Only Arnold can help himself,' said Miss Hendry. 'A few weeks ago he wanted to know something. I didn't think it was time. Now I do. But he doesn't come.'

'Arnold won't do anything,' Peter said. 'He's lost heart. But we thought – Jane and I thought – you might speak to the Duchy agent.'

Miss Hendry considered this for a minute.

'There's only one thing that has any effect on Tom Blackburn,' she said, 'and that's tradition. Arnold's got to establish himself as going back to the year dot. Tom looks after the old tenants. Nobody pushes an old Duchy tenant around if Tom has anything to do with it. Somehow, Arnold needs to get himself under Tom Blackburn's protection.'

'That's what we thought,' said Peter.

'Father to son, that's how the Duchy works as a rule. Now Arnold isn't old Ernest Haithwaite's son. But there are other relationships.'

'Arnold doesn't know who he is.'

'He can find out. Send him to me this morning.'

'I don't think he'll come,' said Peter.

Miss Hendry was silent again for a while. Then she went to a side-table for a telephone directory and copied something from it on to a piece of paper. She folded the paper, put it in an envelope, addressed it to 'Mr Arnold Haithwaite', and handed it to Peter.

'It's an address in Irontown,' she said. 'Tell him to go there.'

'And if he won't?' asked Peter.

'In that case,' said Miss Hendry, 'I'm afraid I can't help him.'

The rain stopped briefly, though there was plenty of it in the sky. Arnold walked home to Cottontree House after spending the morning with the Admiral. The stranger was digging in the little strip of garden at the front. He worked in his own fierce way, attacking the ground like an enemy. As Arnold arrived he threw the spade down and wiped his forehead with a handkerchief.

Arnold hadn't spoken to him for days. But he was curious.

'What do you think you're doing?' he asked.

'Digging a hole.'

'I can see that. But what for?'

'For a post.'

'A post? What sort of a post?'

'Mind your own business,' the man said. Then his tone changed. A note of pride came into his voice. 'If you want to know,' he said, 'I'm putting up a sign-board. I made it myself. You can see it if you like. You'd be seeing it, anyway, soon. I'm just going to get it from the outhouse.'

Sonny led the way to the back. He had painted a board with black and red lettering on a white background. It said:

BAY VIEW PRIVATE HOTEL

Arnold stared.

'Bay View Private Hotel,' he read slowly aloud. 'You mean *here*? You're putting it up in our garden?'

'I am that.'

'Who said you could?'

'I don't need permission from anyone,' the stranger said. 'My uncle's given me a free hand, I do what I like.'

He picked up the post, balanced it for carrying and walked round to the front again. Arnold followed.

'You're daft,' Arnold said. 'This isn't a private hotel, it's just an old house. I mean, it's all very well doing a few bed-and-breakfasts, but if you're going to be a private hotel you need staff. Who's going to run it for you?'

'Aha,' the man said. 'It could well be my wife.'

'Your *wife*? Who's going to marry you?'

The stranger smirked.

'You've met my fiancée,' he said.

'Miss Binns? She walked out. I thought she'd had enough.'

Sonny dropped the post into the hole. He picked up the spade and started shovelling in soil.

'Miss Binns will come round, lad,' he said. 'I saw her in Cobchester the other week. I'll get her back here again, never fear. But I reckon she found everything a bit shabby. She'll like it better when it's smartened up a bit. I've arranged for Mrs Benson to come in and finish that spring-cleaning. And I reckon this sign should make a difference. She'll see that I'm going to run a real business here. Stage One of the marina you might call it. A small start, but it'll show her I'm in earnest.'

He dropped the spade, straightened the post, trampled the ground flat around it.

'There,' he said. 'Looks pretty good, eh?'

He fixed the mobile eye speculatively on Arnold.

'Decided what you're going to do, lad?' he asked. 'If you think it's best for you to go, I won't stand in your way.'

Arnold didn't answer. He was considering the sign-board.

'You're changing the whole place by doing that,' he said.

'Of course I am. That's the idea. Change is what it needs.'

'Bay View!' said Arnold. 'Nobody'll ever call it Bay View. It's Cottontree House. Always has been and always will be.'

'Will it?' said the stranger.

The thought seemed to annoy him.

'Will it, eh?' he said. 'We'll see about that. "Always" is a long time. I never reckoned much to that silly-looking tree, anyroad. It keeps all the light out of the front. Just you hang on a minute.'

He went round to the back again, and reappeared a moment later with the biggest saw from the outhouse.

'Here, what are you up to?' Arnold demanded.

'What do you think?'

'You can't saw that tree down.'

'I can and will.'

'But it's two hundred years old.'

'I don't care if it's two thousand years old.'

Arnold was shocked. It wasn't a light thing to treat old deep-rooted life like that.

He groped for words.

'Listen,' he said. 'That's a rare tree. There isn't another in the Duchy. It came from the West Indies or some such.'

'That makes no difference to me,' Sonny said. 'If it gets in my way I shift it, same as anything else that gets in my way.'

He took up the saw. There was a flurry of large raindrops. Dark, ragged, watery clouds sailed west to east, low in the sky. Peter appeared with Miss Hendry's envelope in his hand. Arnold looked round, saw him, looked back again.

'I've got something for you, Arnold,' Peter said. 'From Miss Hendry. It's an address in Irontown. You've to go there right away.' Peter was full of his own business and didn't really notice what was going on.

'Stop and think about it,' Arnold urged the stranger. 'Don't do something daft in a hurry. You'll be sorry if you do.'

' "Woodman, spare that tree," ' the man said. There was the ghost of a smile on his face. 'Who's going to stop me? You? You feel like trying another fight?'

'Arnold!' Peter said. 'Miss Hendry says, if you want to find out who you are, to go to this address in Irontown. And you'd better go today. Right away.'

'Oh, hop it!' said Arnold impatiently. He called to the man again: 'Put that saw down!'

But Sonny wasn't putting it down. Seeing Arnold upset was obviously giving him an unexpected pleasure. He took his time, ran his finger along the teeth of the saw, then moved the saw up and down the trunk, choosing a place to start cutting.

'Shall I go instead of you?' Peter said in Arnold's ear.

'Go where?'

'To this address in Irontown that Miss Hendry gave me.'

'Go where you like but leave me alone,' said Arnold. Then, to the man, 'For the last time, put down that saw!'

'Come on, make me!' Sonny said.

Arnold grabbed at the hand that held the saw. There was a scuffle. No one saw it, for Peter was already heading away up the street. It lasted only a minute. Then Arnold was on the ground. He picked himself up. This time he wasn't unmarked, for the saw had caught his shin.

'That was an accident,' Sonny said, the grating voice very soft. 'You brought it on yourself.' There was a little blood on the saw, and the man took out a white handkerchief and wiped the blade carefully. Blood trickled too from the cut on Arnold's shin and soaked into his plimsolls.

The man chose his place and drew the saw two or three times across the trunk of the cotton tree.

'A blunt old thing, this,' he complained. 'Rusty, too. I can't think why you haven't got a better saw. At least you could have maintained this one properly. It wouldn't do for *me*, I can tell you.'

Arnold, outraged, sought in vain for a reply. The saw rasped and squeaked and a bit of bark fell off the tree-trunk. Then the rain crashed down. Arnold and Sonny took refuge in the only near-by place, which was the front doorway of Cottontree House.

They stood side by side, uncomfortably close together. The cloud-burst lasted five minutes. The high street became a small river. Then the downpour eased into heavy rain. Heavy rain became light rain. Then it stopped, though the sky stayed grey and threatening.

The man stepped from the doorway. Water stood on the trodden soil where he'd been digging, and his post was surrounded by a little pool. He still held the saw, but didn't seem in a hurry to continue.

'I'll have to get another saw,' he said. 'With this one of yours it'd take me all day.'

'That's right, give it a rest,' said Arnold. 'Then you might think better of it.'

'Oh no,' the man said. He half smiled. 'I don't give things up, lad. Haven't you noticed? That's not my way at all. But I don't rush. I can take my time.'

He smiled again, more broadly.

'Given the proper tools,' he said, 'I can make any job a pleasure. I shall enjoy this one.'

The good eye studied Arnold with a mixture of malice and satisfaction.

'I hope you're not disappointed, lad,' Sonny said. 'You can watch me another day. And in the meantime you'll be able to look forward to it. If you behave yourself I might even let you do a bit.'

'Blast you!' Arnold said, and added other words.

'Naughty, naughty,' said the man. Arnold knew Sonny was trying to goad him into lashing out again. There was no point in staying any longer. The rain was starting up again, but he didn't want to go indoors. He turned up the collar of his cape and stumped away into the main street.

Chapter Twenty-three

Peter cycled out of the manor-house drive and almost bumped into Arnold. Arnold would have gone past, but Peter stopped him. Peter spoke guiltily.

'Arnold,' he said, 'I opened that envelope.'

'What envelope?'

'The one Miss Hendry gave me.'

'I don't know what you're talking about.'

'It's only a few minutes since I was telling you,' Peter said patiently. 'Miss Hendry gave me an envelope with an address in it. She said, if you want to find out who you are, that's where you should go. And I reckon the time to find out is today, because the Duchy agent's coming to see Miss Hendry tonight, and if anyone can help you he can. And I thought . . .' Peter hesitated, then went on, 'I thought, if you weren't going to take any notice, perhaps I ought to do something about it myself. So I opened it.'

Peter waited for Arnold's anger. Opening a letter addressed to someone else, even with good intentions, was contrary to all his codes of behaviour, and he felt ashamed. But Arnold showed no sign of resentment.

'Let's have a look,' he said.

Peter felt in his pocket and silently handed over the piece of paper.

'Mavis, Hair Stylist, 23 Fore Street, Irontown.' That was all it said, in Miss Hendry's tall, angular handwriting.

'Doesn't mean a thing to me,' said Arnold. He handed it back.

'I didn't really think it would,' said Peter.

Arnold made as if to move on.

'Arnold, surely you're interested? I mean, this is important to you, it *must* be. You were interested a few weeks ago. Why not now?'

'Oh, I don't know,' Arnold said. He couldn't have explained. He felt buffeted by events, felt that nothing mattered any more, felt that Sonny was in possession now and wouldn't be shifted. And the fate of the cotton tree disturbed him more deeply than he could understand. That would be the last, decisive blow. If that went it couldn't be put back and nothing could be the same again whatever happened.

'Well, if you don't mind,' said Peter, 'I shall go and see what I can find out. But it may not be any good. People often won't tell things if it's just a boy asking.'

'Here, give me it again,' Arnold said.

He looked at the paper once more. 'Mavis, Hair Stylist, 23 Fore Street, Irontown.' And this time, in spite of everything, interest stirred in him – interest mixed with apprehension.

'It might be . . .' he said, and stopped in mid-sentence, staggered by the size of the thought that struck him. 'It might be my . . .'

'Well, yes, it might, mightn't it?' said Peter.

'How'm I going to get to Irontown?'

'Same way as me. Bicycle.'

'I haven't got one.'

'Borrow Jane's.'

'What, a girl's bicycle?'

'For heaven's sake, Arnold,' said Peter, 'Don't you know what's important and what isn't? Borrow *any* bike. But Jane's is nearest. She's out today. She won't mind.'

They got Jane's bicycle from the coach-house. It was an ordinary black roadster, just a means of getting from one place to another. They had to raise the saddle and pump up the tyres before Arnold could use it. By the time they were ready to cycle up the hill out of Skirlston, his interest was turning into scepticism.

'That address won't mean anything,' he said. 'When it comes to the point, we'll just have been wasting our time.'

'Have you anything else to do with your time?' Peter asked.

Arnold hadn't. He said no more, and rode on. The wind had got stronger and was behind them, giving a little help. But it was a long pull out of the village, and they had to walk the last quarter of a mile. From the top of the hill and round Skirl Head to

Irontown was an up-and-down ride, the 'downs' being mostly brief swoops, perilous on a wet road, while the 'ups' seemed to go on for ever. Spells of rain grew more frequent. Arnold trudged or pedalled silently. By the time they reached the first streets of Irontown Peter's legs were aching and he was wondering what he was doing all this for.

Irontown had grown first from the iron mines, then from the blast-furnaces. It was a small port, too, with some coastal trade. It shipped coal and cement – both of which you could sometimes taste in the air – from Workville, five miles farther north, which had no harbour. It was an ugly, smoky town, but it was redeemed a little by the sea below and the fells above. Arnold knew where Fore Street was. It was right down on the quay, and the only difficulty was that they had to half ride, half slide with brakes on, down a series of cobbled streets.

At the bottom the harbour was square and almost enclosed; the water an odd, thick-looking grey, fringed with detergent foam and a good deal of litter. There was one ship tied up at the far side, and a steam-engine fussed with a line of trucks along the quay. A row of small shops looked across at this scene, with MAVIS, HAIR STYLIST in the middle – on its left a café with prices painted in

white on the windows, on its right a secondhand-magazine shop. Mavis's was the most modern, with the name over the door picked out in large green plastic letters.

Arnold and Peter propped up their bicycles against the kerb. Arnold spoke for the first time for half an hour.

'You go first,' he said.

'Don't you think it would be better if you did?' said Peter. 'Or at least if we went in together? I mean, you're older, and after all, this is all *about* you, isn't it?'

But now the time had come Arnold seemed apprehensive. He shifted uneasily from one foot to the other, looking out over the harbour and not meeting Peter's eye.

'Maybe I'll not bother after all,' he said. 'Maybe it's best left alone.'

'What, when we've come all this way?'

'Well, I ... well, it's been a long time, and I'm not good at meeting folks. That's if there's anyone to meet.'

'We'd better find out, hadn't we?' said Peter. 'All right, I'll be first. Stand clear of the door in case I come flying out on my ear. Here goes.'

He took a deep breath and pushed the door open, trying to look more confident than he felt. The shop was smart enough inside. Four or five women sat under driers. Another was having her hair waved by an assistant. At a desk behind a cash register sat a large, dark, solid woman, her hair-style twenty years younger than the rest of her. She was smoking, and chattering at long range to the most distant of the customers. Everyone looked at Peter as he went in. This was feminine territory.

'Are you Mavis?' Peter asked the woman at the cash desk.

She looked at him, blew out smoke, took her time.

'Yes,' she said at length. 'I'm Mavis. You can call me Mrs Greenwood if you like.'

'Miss Hendry suggested I should see you,' Peter said. 'Miss Hendry from Skirlston.'

'Miss Hendry,' said Mavis. There was no telling whether the name meant anything to her. 'She doesn't come here.'

'Happen the lad wants his hair permed,' said one of the customers. Two or three others laughed. Peter reddened. Mavis took no notice of the witticism.

'Well,' she said, 'what do you want?'

'It's – it's sort of private,' Peter said.

'Nothing's private here,' said Mavis.

'She can say that again,' said the witty customer. 'They'll tell you anything here. Amazing what you learn.'

'No place for a lad,' said another customer. She giggled. All were welcoming Peter as a diversion.

'I came to ask you about somebody,' Peter said.

'Ask away,' said Mavis.

'It's about Arnold Haithwaite.'

The reaction was barely noticeable, but it was there. Mavis drew a little harder on her cigarette. Her eyebrows moved fractionally together. There was a moment's awareness in her eyes. Then she said:

'Never heard of him.'

Peter drew himself up straight and took a chance.

'I think you have,' he said.

He thought for a moment he was going to be sent packing.
Then Mavis said:

'Half a minute. Yes, you're right, I have. A long time ago.' She
stood up.

'Miss Hendry sent you, you said. I don't know what my
memory's coming to. What's your name?'

'Peter Ellison.'

'That's right. She told me you were coming and I forgot all
about it. I've got the thing she sent you for. It's at the back there.
Mary, keep an eye on things for a few minutes, will you? Follow
me, lad, through the shop.'

Peter followed to a room at the back. It was small, dark, but
brightly furnished, contemporary. Rain beat on the window.
Mavis closed the door behind him.

'Did Miss Hendry really tell you I was coming?' Peter asked.

'No. They're all inquisitive, that's all. I never let them think
there's anything unexpected happening.'

She looked at him hard.

'Now,' she said, 'what's all this about Arnold Haithwaite?'

'I want to know who he really is, that's all.'

Mavis put out her cigarette, slowly.

'What's it got to do with you?' she asked. 'Or with Miss
Hendry? And why did she send you, instead of coming herself?'

Peter hadn't really any answers.

'I think perhaps she . . . didn't like to come here herself,' he said,
chancing his arm.

'Could be,' the woman said. 'Could be. These old spinsters.
Well, if Miss Hendry thinks I'm going to talk about it to a lad
your age, she's got another think coming. Anything Miss Hendry
wants to know from me, she can come and ask me herself. Tell her
that.'

Peter had to play his last card.

'As a matter of fact,' he said, 'Arnold Haithwaite's with me
now. Just out there in the street.'

'Oh.'

Mavis sat down on a sofa. Slowly and thoughtfully she lit another cigarette. Then she said:

'All right, bring him in. Not through the shop. Go out the back door, through the yard and round the block. And bring him in the same way.'

When Peter came back with Arnold she was still sitting on the sofa. She nodded to Arnold, motioned him to a chair in the corner, but didn't show any sign of welcome or recognition.

'So you don't know who he is,' she said, addressing Peter. 'In that case you don't know much. Well, let me tell you one thing right away. It wasn't me.'

'I don't know what you mean,' Peter said.

'It wasn't me, it was her. My sister. Beryl.'

'What happened?'

'What happened? Come off it, lad. Even if you don't know much about it you must have heard something, or you wouldn't be here. You can't be *quite* as innocent as you look. What do you think happened? My sister kept company with young Haithwaite, the one that died. Frank. She had a baby, that's what happened. Women do have babies, in case you didn't know.'

She pointed towards the corner.

'Him,' she said. 'For what it's worth, he's my nephew.'

Then she spoke to Arnold for the first time.

'But don't start making anything of it,' she said. 'I don't want auntying at this stage. It's too late. Far too late.'

'You must have known,' Arnold said slowly. 'You must have known I was at Skirlston.'

'Oh yes,' said Mavis. 'At least, I supposed you were. But don't blame me for not taking an interest. Blame old man Haithwaite for that. He didn't want to know us.'

'And what about Arnold's . . . mother?' Peter asked.

'She left him on the doorstep. Well, not exactly on the doorstep, that's a figure of speech. She left him in a carry-cot in the out-house and put a note through the letter-box to say she'd gone. And so she had. They never saw her again.'

Arnold didn't seem to be listening. He'd got up from the chair and was peering through the rain-blurred window, though there was nothing beyond it but the backyard.

Mavis's eyes narrowed.

'What's all this about?' she asked after a minute. 'Why do you want to know now? All these years afterwards. What's in it for who?'

'What's in it,' said Peter frankly, 'is a Duchy tenancy. Or could be. If Arnold was old Mr Haithwaite's son it might help him. But I dare say being his grandson is just as good.'

'I dare say,' Mavis said. There was a slight dryness in her tone. Peter couldn't account for it.

'It seems funny to me,' he said, 'that there should be such a mystery over it.'

'Shame, you know,' Mavis said. 'The Haithwaites were respectable folk. They didn't like having a thing like this happening in their family. And it was a few years back, when these sort of matters weren't talked about.'

'But Arnold isn't a child. He could have been told by now.'

Mavis stubbed out her cigarette.

'There was something else,' she said at length. 'Young Haithwaite said the kiddie wasn't his. There was quite a to-do about it. But they kept him in the end.'

'And was he?' Peter asked.

'Well, if you want to know, I reckon he wasn't. She had another friend, too. A sailor. It was him she went off with, to Cardiff. She didn't want the kiddie. I think young Frank was took in. He paid the price and a bit more. But mind you, I don't know. Nobody knows for sure, or ever will.'

Arnold spoke at last, without looking round.

'Where is she?' he asked.

'You tell me,' Mavis said. 'I heard from her five years ago. She was in Liverpool then. I'll hear from her again some day, I dare say. If she wants money.'

'And . . . him?'

'The one she ran off with? You remind me of him, now I come to think of it. I don't know what became of him. She finished with him long ago. He could be anywhere in the world, or out of it for that matter.'

In the silence that followed, the last sentence seemed to hang in the air.

'Now listen, both of you,' Mavis said. 'I've told you what I know, but this has nothing to do with me, nothing. You understand that? When the Haithwaites took in Beryl's kiddie they took the responsibility and nobody else is having it now, least of all me. I don't want to get involved in anything. And now if you don't mind I'll ask you to go out the back way and let me get back to the shop. You can't trust these assistants. Customers tell them some tale or other and get out without paying. You've no idea. It's a hard world for some of us, and that's a fact.'

Peter and Arnold pushed their bicycles up through the cobbled streets of Irontown to the main road at the top. A mile away the way to Skirlston a lane turned off for Solithwaite, high in the fells. Arnold stopped, and spoke for the first time since leaving Mavis's premises.

'I'm going up to see Arch Rawson at Brow Farm,' he said. 'He wants an answer to a question. I might as well give him it. I'll be a good half-hour.'

'I'll wait for you,' Peter said. 'Or come with you if you like. Just as you wish.'

'No.'

Arnold's wasn't an expressive face, but today Peter could read it well enough, and didn't argue. He knew Arnold wanted neither speech nor company. Without a word he got on his bicycle and pedalled away towards Skirlston, leaving Arnold to take the Solithwaite side-road.

The rain wasn't continuous. It came in gusts, carried on the wind, almost horizontal. Grey clouds ran, ragged and rapid, across the sky. Down on Peter's right the sea was indigo, flecked with white horses. As he rounded the headland the wind came at him more fiercely, caught his cape like a sail, changed his course, twice nearly blew him off. It would be safer to walk, but Peter didn't feel like walking. In the wild, swooping ride round Skirl Bay was a desolation that matched his mood. Words wheeled in his mind like sea-gulls in the air. '. . . Could be anywhere in the world, or out of it for that matter . . . Nothing to do with me, nothing . . .'

Where the road crossed the River Skirl there was a hold-up.

Heavy lorries laden with sandbags were crawling into and out of the narrow gravel track that led down to the old railway viaduct. They swung wide for the sharp turn, blocking the road totally. Two police cars were there, lights flashing in warning. Traffic was held up, now this way, now that way, now both ways. Under the bridge the Skirl ran fast and high.

Peter got through after a few minutes, pedalled on. When the road turned west for Skirlston, the wind was in his face. His legs felt weak, too weak to shift the machine. But it kept moving all

the same. He had the illusion that the wheels were driving him, that the pedals were turning his feet. Even on the last long hill down into the village, the wind in his cape cancelled out the steep slope. His brakes were untouched; the pedals still went round. 'Could be anywhere in the world, or out of it for that matter ... Nothing to do with me, nothing ...'

Peter turned into the manor-house drive and was suddenly sheltered, realizing afresh the strength of the wind by the difference when it stopped. He left the bicycle in the coach-house, hung his cape in the porch and went into the house. It was warm in there; safe from the buffetings outside.

'I hope you did what you set out to do,' Helen Ellison said. 'Whatever it was.'

Peter didn't tell her anything.

'Mr Blackburn's arrived already,' his mother went on after a minute. 'That's the Duchy agent. He's dining with Miss Hendry, you know. I haven't really *seen* him, of course, except a glimpse through the window. He went straight round to the Wing. He seemed to know his way. I suppose there's no reason why he should call on us, we've never been introduced, but still ...'

'I'd like a hot drink,' Peter said.

'I'll make you a cup of tea ... Goodness, it's well after seven already. We'll be eating in less than an hour. I wish Jane and Jeremy would come, it's not like them to be late and they said they'd be here by now.'

'Where are they?'

'Out for the day. In Jeremy's car.'

'They're probably airborne by now.'

'It is rather windy, isn't it?' Helen said.

'That,' said Peter, 'is a prize understatement.'

'I'm glad she's with Jeremy, he's so reliable. Still, I wish they'd come. These young people don't realize that one worries about them. Even Jane and Jeremy can lack consideration.'

Peter switched on the radio.

'That was the Tykes,' a voice said, 'asking "Don't we all love her?" To which the answer of course is "Yes". And now, before we continue on Radio One, a gale warning. The Admiralty issued the following warning at 19.00 hours to all shipping in the sea areas Rockall, Shannon, Fastnet, Malin, Irish Sea and Skirl Head: westerly gale, force nine, imminent. I'd better repeat that: westerly gale, force nine, imminent in sea areas Rockall, Shannon, Fastnet, Malin, Irish Sea and Skirl Head. And now, it seems a long time since we last heard Dawn Golden in this programme, twenty minutes at least . . .'

Peter switched off.

'I *said* it was windy,' said Helen Ellison. 'I do wish Jane and Jeremy would come . . . You know, really you'd think Mr Blackburn was the Prince himself, the fuss that's made about him. And I'd like to see either him or the Prince build a nuclear power-station.'

There was a tap on the door.

'Peter!' Miss Hendry called. 'Peter! Can you spare a minute? I'd like you to have a word with Mr Blackburn.'

'Off you go, Peter,' said Helen Ellison. 'Some of us are privileged to meet the great. Others must rely on reports. I shall look to you for a full account later.'

Arnold left Jane's bicycle alongside Peter's in the coach-house and walked, head down, through the village and up to the Admiral's house.

'Well,' he said, 'I'm on my way. I've got a job.'

'Where, lad?'

'Arch Rawson's, over at Solithwaite.'

'Rawson of Brow Farm?' said the Admiral. 'You'll be all right there. I'll be sorry to see you go, mind you. Sorrier than you think. But you could have done much worse. I've known Arch Rawson since he was a lad. And his dad before him. A good farm and honest folk, and you can't ask more than that. When are you leaving Skirlston?'

'Tomorrow.'

'Tomorrow? That's quick.'

'It can't be too quick for me.'

'Aye, well,' said the Admiral, 'things being as they are, it's maybe all for the best. I hope you'll be happy there. Mind you, it rains at Solithwaite. It's the way them fells are shaped. And wind, it fair funnels in. But there, we've no room to talk about wind and rain in Skirlston, have we? – on a night like this, an' all.'

'Highest tide of the year tonight,' said Arnold.

'Aye. And not just that. With a west wind like this to bring it in, and all the water there is in the Skirl, there'll be floods, big floods.'

'You don't need to tell me that,' said Arnold. 'Or anyone else. They've been driving the sheep off the dunes, down Red Bank way. And sandbagging the old viaduct.'

'You know, lad,' the Admiral said, 'after sixty-eight years in Skirlston I still find it exciting, a night like this. You've picked a right day for your last at Cottontree House. Maybe we should be celebrating. How about a drop of last year's cowslip? Or – wait a minute – aye, I will, I believe I will. I'll tap the '73 damson. Been three years in a rum barrel that has, Arnold lad. It'll be like red rum, now.'

'I don't feel much like celebrating,' Arnold said.

'I suppose not,' said the Admiral. He changed the subject. 'I might go down and have a look myself later on,' he said.

'Then you'd better not start on the damson till after,' Arnold said.

'When will it be in, do you reckon? The tide?'

'Twenty minutes early on this wind, that's what I'd say.'

'And that's what I'd say, too. Which makes it half past eight. Not much more than an hour from now. Staying for some supper with me, lad?'

'I'm not hungry. I'll go and get my things packed, ready for tomorrow. See you later on, Joe.'

The Admiral went with Arnold to the gate. It was raining again, and the light was starting to fail.

'I wouldn't like to be down there on the bay tonight,' the Admiral said.

'Nobody will be,' said Arnold, 'that isn't out of their wits.'

Chapter Twenty-four

Peter followed Miss Hendry along the passageway that led to her sitting-room. Mr Blackburn, the Duchy agent, was seated in an armchair in front of the gas fire. He raised himself a few inches in token courtesy, then sank back again. He was a heavy man, had been a Rugby footballer in his day; had been a colonel, too, though he didn't like to be addressed by the rank. His hair was thick and grey, and curled over his ears. His eyes were blue, his face a beefy red. He had a glass at his elbow.

'This is the boy I told you about,' Miss Hendry said. 'In connection with the Haithwaite business.'

'Oh yes, the Haithwaite business,' Mr Blackburn said. His voice was surprisingly light, his accent the Oxford accent of the older generation. He covered up a yawn.

'Now pay attention, Tom,' Miss Hendry commanded him.

'My dear Katharine, I *always* pay attention,' Mr Blackburn said.

Peter was shocked that anyone should dare to address Miss Hendry by her first name. In fact, it had hardly occurred to him until that moment that she had one.

'As I was telling you earlier on, Tom,' Miss Hendry said, 'old Ernest Haithwaite . . .'

'Dear old Ernest,' interjected Mr Blackburn.

'. . . Old Ernest Haithwaite, who's lived in Cottontree House all his life, has been there alone with this boy Arnold since his wife died six years ago. And Arnold – as I think Peter knows by now, but if he doesn't it had still better be said – is the old man's grandson, though for reasons of respectability it was never acknowledged.'

'Well, actually . . .' Peter began. But Miss Hendry didn't stop.

'And then a few weeks ago this strange character appeared on the scene, claiming to be the old man's nephew. And a very un-likely claim it seems to be. And Peter found that this man, when he's at home, lives in some incredible derelict attic in Cobchester. He doesn't seem to belong anywhere or to anyone. But he took the old man in completely.'

'And Mr Haithwaite took *him* in,' said Peter, 'and he's living there now. And it looks as if Arnold will be out, if he doesn't get murdered or something first.'

'Come now,' said Mr Blackburn.

'Don't be melodramatic, Peter,' said Miss Hendry. 'Anyway, Tom, that's what it's all about. Here's Arnold, who's lived in Skirlston ever since he was born, apparently being pushed out by this odd and unpleasant person from nowhere. And we think you ought to stop it.'

'Me?' said Mr Blackburn.

'Yes, you.'

'But, my dear Katharine,' Mr Blackburn said, 'we're not – re-grettably, perhaps – living in the eighteenth century. The Duchy doesn't order people's lives for them any more.'

'Oh, come off it, Tom,' Miss Hendry said. 'Of course the Duchy orders people's lives for them. You tell them what to do and they do it.'

'And you expect me to tell old Ernest Haithwaite who he can and can't have in his house?'

'Yes.'

'On pain of losing his Duchy tenancy, I suppose?'

'Yes.'

'I wonder why anyone ever called women the gentle sex. They're much more ruthless than men. I wouldn't dream of doing such a thing to poor old Ernest. Anyway, you seem to forget, my dear, that a Duchy tenancy is controlled by modern legislation, like any other.'

'Controlled at a rent of one bunch of wild violets per annum?'

'Precisely. Controlled at a rent of one bunch of wild violets – which his Royal Highness doesn't actually insist on.'

'Tom, you're stalling,' said Miss Hendry. 'You know very well you only have to tell old Ernest "That man goes out!" and out he'll go. And I want you to do it. After all, tradition is everything to the Duchy, and blood's thicker than water, and Haithwaites have been at Cottontree House for the last two hundred years, and Arnold is the old man's grandson, the last of the line.'

'Well, actually ...' Peter began again. He'd been hesitating, afraid that what he had to say might put an end to Arnold's chances. But Peter had the instincts of the true researcher. If you sought for the truth and found it, your duty was to tell it. He told it.

'As a matter of fact,' he said, 'nobody knows who Arnold's father really was, but he was probably a seaman from Cardiff.' And he told them of his conversation with Mavis, hair-stylist.

Before he'd finished, Mr Blackburn was drumming with his fingers on the edge of his chair. He was bored with the subject of the Haithwaites. Peter hurried nervously on to the end of his story.

'Anyway,' he said, trying to retrieve something for Arnold from the wreckage of his Haithwaite ancestry, 'that fellow's no more a Haithwaite than he is. And he does some ridiculous things. Do you know, he's put up a sign saying "Bay View Private Hotel"...'

'He's what?'

Mr Blackburn sat up with a jerk.

'He's put up a sign saying "Bay View Private Hotel",' Peter repeated.

'But he can't,' said Mr Blackburn. 'Not in Skirlston. Not while I'm around, he can't.'

'My dear Tom,' said Miss Hendry, sweetly and a shade maliciously, 'so long as old Ernest pays his rent of one bunch of wild violets per annum he's a protected tenant. The Duchy can't order people's lives for them. We're not in the eighteenth century.'

'Oh, balderdash,' said Mr Blackburn. 'I'm not having that, I can tell you. Bay View Private Hotel. It'll be a skittle alley next.'

'And he says he's cutting down the cotton tree,' said Peter.

This time Mr Blackburn stood up straight.

'He's – cutting – down – ? Nonsense, boy, nobody would dare to do that.'

'Well, that's what he says.'

'I can't believe it!' said Mr Blackburn. He stalked to the french window, looked out at the rain for a moment, walked back and stood over Peter.

'You're having me on, aren't you?' he said.

'I'm not having you on,' said Peter. 'He was just starting to do it this morning. You don't know him. He might do *anything*.'

'Anything else,' said Mr Blackburn, 'but not that! Why, the man's mad. Crazy. There's not another tree like that in the North of England!'

He was agitated now. Miss Hendry quietly took the glass from his hand. It dawned on Peter that a tenancy dispute was routine to Mr Blackburn, and boring routine at that. But a private hotel sign in Skirlston, and still more the threat to the cotton tree – these, in the agent's eyes, were things that mattered.

'Where's my coat, Katharine?' he said. 'I'm going down there right away. I'll tell the fellow myself. I won't stand for it.'

'There's a meal waiting for you, Tom,' Miss Hendry said. 'Go and see him later.'

'I'll go and see him *now*!' said Mr Blackburn.

'You'll be in a better temper when you've had some dinner.'

'I don't *want* to be in a better temper,' Mr Blackburn said. 'Cut down the cotton tree indeed. Cut down the cotton tree! I'll cut *him* down to size, you see if I don't. I'll have him on the way back to Cobchester with his tail between his legs, double quick!'

He was struggling into his topcoat.

'Do come back and have your dinner soon, Tom,' Miss Hendry said.

Mr Blackburn muttered something, strode to the french window, opened it and disappeared into the rain. Peter and Miss Hendry looked at each other.

'Well!' Miss Hendry said. 'That certainly had its effect! I wish I'd known, Peter – I could have told you right away that the cotton tree would make him move if nothing else did. I can hardly believe it myself. Surely even that dreadful man wouldn't dare . . .?'

'I wouldn't like to be in his shoes tonight,' said Peter. 'It's a good job Mr Blackburn hasn't a horsewhip!'

'Well, you weren't with the great man for long, Peter,' said

Helen Ellison. 'A brief encounter indeed. Though more than your parents had. What did you talk about?'

'Oh, about Arnold, mostly, and the man who's staying at his house.'

'How odd. How very odd ... I do wish Jane and Jeremy would come. They should have been here twenty minutes ago, and it's not like them to be late. And on a night like this ... You talked about *Arnold*, you said? The boy who came to tea here in a navy serge suit? And the man – the one I see around the village in a black beret?'

Peter nodded.

'Not the most enthralling of topics, I'd have thought,' said his mother. 'You disappoint me, Peter. I wondered what marvellous things you'd hear. After all, Mr Blackburn is the Prince's right-hand man. He must have something more interesting to talk about than Skirlston gossip. I was all agog. I longed to bask, as they say, in reflected glory ... Oh dear, I do wish Jane and Jeremy would come.'

Chapter Twenty-five

'Not that place again!' Jeremy said. 'I don't know what you find so attractive about it.'

'Nor do I,' said Jane. 'It appeals to me, that's all.'

'We're late already, remember.'

'Late for what? We're not catching a train.'

'Late for supper, of course.'

'In some people's eyes,' said Jane, 'life revolves round the table. Not in mine.'

'Oh, Jane, you are *hopeless*,' Jeremy said. But he turned the MG down towards St Brendan's Church.

Jeremy had a roundish face, a fair skin, blue eyes, a few freckles, sandy hair. Jeremy was patient. He thought Jane a wayward, unpredictable creature. She knew it, and sometimes played up, but she didn't think it of herself.

Down on the dunes the wind blew wild and salty. Jeremy stopped the car. Jane jumped out and ran towards the causeway, her hair streaming out like a banner. Jeremy followed without enthusiasm.

She was half-way across to the church when he reached the landward end of the causeway. She stopped, flung her arms wide in a mock balancing act, turned, ran back to him, nearly bore him over. She swung round, took his arm, led him on again over the causeway. With what breath she had she was laughing, laughing all the way.

The church – but it was no church now, it had long been deconsecrated – was bare, deserted, bleak. It was only a shell, but a shell of enormous strength, a shell whose walls were four feet thick, a shell of Skirlston stone. It was a shell that did strange things to sound. On days when the wind wasn't strong your footsteps echoed threefold, so that one person could sound like a party. Today all echoes were drowned. The wind whistled through the paneless windows, its note changing with its direction, changing from window to window, the music of a mad organist.

The church was a thousand years old.

Jeremy didn't like it at any time. Even in calm, sunny weather it was cold inside, and skeletal. The walls were limewashed, and pencilled with countless indecencies. Outside, the tiny island on which the church stood was really a graveyard. The deaths it recorded were by drowning only. Some were of men whose ships had foundered or been wrecked on Skirl Head, or who had been swept overboard in gales. Some were of men, women and children overtaken by the tide on Skirl sands. None were of the twentieth century.

But this was no time for reading the inscriptions on gravestones. The rain had paused but the wind still blew hard and the light was fading. Jane and Jeremy walked once round the outside of the church, once round the inside. Jeremy shivered. He put his lips to Jane's ear, because you couldn't speak to anyone naturally against the competition of the wind.

'Satisfied?' he shouted.

Jane stood on tiptoe and replied in the same way.

'Not yet.'

'We ought to be going. It's long past the time we said we'd be back.'

'It's what?'

'It's late. We're late!'

'But Jeremy! It's fun here!'

'What? What did you say?'

'Fun!'

'Not to me it isn't.'

'I wish we could get up into the tower and watch the tide coming in. But there's no way up.'

'Oh, come *on*!' Even Jeremy was getting impatient.

'I'm just going to stand on that wall a minute.'

In front of them was the dilapidated remnant of a wall that had once encircled the island. Jane climbed up on it. Jeremy followed reluctantly and stood beside her.

'There you are!' Jane shouted. 'The sea. Right out there!' She was excited again.

Jeremy looked. There was still a wide expanse of sand to the west of the church. But beyond it you could see the sea. It didn't seem to be moving.

'Satisfied now?' he called.

'Not quite. It doesn't look as if it was coming in, does it? But it's sort of getting bigger. Seems silly, doesn't it, the sea getting bigger?'

'That's the angle you're watching it from. But look, you can see it's moving now.'

Then, suddenly, it was coming, driven by the wind, not in successive waves like every other sea they had ever seen, but just one single wave, sweeping on, as fast as a galloping horse. In a few seconds acres of sand disappeared, as if wiped away by a sponge. In a few more seconds there wasn't even the wave to be seen. All was water now between the church and the higher sands over at Skirlston, and the tide was racing on towards the railway viaduct.

The church was an island again, except for the causeway, two or three feet above water-level, which still linked it to the shore.

'Come on!' Jeremy yelled. 'Come on, before the causeway's under water too!'

'It's high tide now, it must be. It only comes round the church for a few minutes twice a year. I want to wait and see it go out again.'

Jeremy jumped from the wall, pulled her down, tried to tug her towards the causeway. Jane was furious.

'*You* go if you like!' she shouted.

'All right, I will.'

Jeremy set off across the causeway. The water was still rising, had risen while they were arguing. Waves broke against it on the seaward side. One of them showered him with spray.

Near the far end Jeremy turned back, as he had intended to do if she didn't follow. Another breaker flung spray high as a tree, wetting him again. Close to the church, water crossed the causeway, running swift and shallow.

Jane changed her mind quickly, decided to come. She snatched off her sneakers, shoved them in her anorak pockets, rolled her slacks above the knees. She and Jeremy trudged towards each other. The causeway was only intermittently above water now. It was a shape, a sea-monster, half-submerged. The wind still blew, the air grew greyer, daylight had nearly gone.

Thirty yards apart, they stopped. There was only water between them. The causeway must still be there, they'd be all right if they kept on it, it ran straight from one to the other. But you couldn't see, you couldn't *see*. And if you stepped off it now . . .

'Go back!' they yelled to each other in the same moment. And both had the sense to retreat. There was water between Jane and the church too, but the distance was short. She felt her way step by step, taking her time in spite of mounting fear. The wind was pushing her off the causeway. Once she put a foot where the causeway wasn't, but she drew it back, and knowledge of the edge helped her get fresh bearings. And then she was there, stubbing her toe on the first of the three stone steps that rose from the causeway to the island.

Even the island's surface was only a foot or two above water-level. From the grass and the flourishing weeds around the gravestones you wouldn't think the island had been under water for years. It was going under now.

Jeremy was on the shore. Jane could just pick out his figure in the gloom, could see that he was waving. He might be shouting, too, but if he was she couldn't hear a word. She wondered if the flatlands where he stood would be flooded, too.

Jane leaned against the wall she had been standing on a few minutes earlier. She didn't want to go inside the dark church. She couldn't see Jeremy any more. Then the car headlights came on, flashed on and off, on and off in some kind of message. The flashing stopped. The car moved, turned, showed its tail-lamps. The two spots of red dwindled and disappeared. Jeremy had gone. Probably water was threatening him and the car by now. There was nothing he could do by staying, anyway. And none of this was his fault. If he had had his way they'd have been warm and dry in Skirlston Manor now, just sitting down to their dinner.

But calling herself a fool didn't help. When all sight and sound of the car had gone, her panic doubled and redoubled. She was here alone with wind and tide. Water washed round her feet and over the gravestones. In another five minutes there wouldn't be any island, there would only be the church. Jane abandoned the wall and went reluctantly inside. It was noisier there than outside, for the wind bounced and howled around as if in the depths of some monstrous instrument.

She told herself that she wasn't in danger. The tide would turn any minute, and meanwhile she was perfectly safe in the church. But none of these thoughts seemed much of a prop against the elements.

She found she was shouting out, shouting at the top of her voice, shouting into the darkness. 'I'm scared!' she shouted. 'Scared, scared, scared!'

Chapter Twenty-six

On his way back to Cottontree House from the Admiral's, Arnold paused to lean over the railings of Skirlston Quay. The tide wasn't here yet, but it would come, and with this wind behind it it would come in fast. Although he was leaving, although he'd told himself twenty times he didn't care any more about anything that happened in Skirlston, he still felt a professional interest. He wanted to see it.

But there was time to pack his things first. And he'd have to say some kind of farewell to the old man. He hadn't seen Ernest Haithwaite since the day Sonny moved in. He hadn't wanted to see him, he was still resentful, he felt it was partly the old man's fault he was having to leave. Yet at the same time he had a sense of guilt, because he knew that Ernest must have missed him and would miss him more when he had gone.

With a mixture of thoughts and feelings, none of them pleasant, Arnold trudged up the main street towards the house. As he approached it a big car came splashing down from the other direction. A man leaped out of it, strode to the front door, tugged at the old-fashioned bell-pull. Nothing happened. The man knocked on the door, hard. Still nothing happened. He hammered at the door with both fists and gave it a kick, but there was still no response. Then he turned swiftly, strode back towards his car and saw Arnold.

'Here, you!' he said. The tone was one of command. The Duchy agent was used to being listened to.

Arnold went up to him slowly, saying nothing. Mr Blackburn peered into his face.

'Are you the Haithwaite lad?' he demanded.

Arnold was inclined to reply that he didn't know or care who he was. But he didn't. There was no point even in that. He nodded.

'Why doesn't anyone come?' the agent said. 'Where's Ernest? Where's that fellow? He's the one I want to see. The one who says he's going to cut down the cotton tree.'

'You mean Sonny,' Arnold said. 'I don't know where he is.'

Mr Blackburn stalked over to the tree, found the place on the trunk where the saw had been drawn across, felt it gently with his fingers.

'The rogue!' he said. 'I won't have it, I tell you I won't have it. And as for that . . .'

He marched up to the BAY VIEW PRIVATE HOTEL sign, bent his broad shoulders, heaved it from the ground, and threw it flat on its back.

'Don't let him dare replace it!' he said, and then, 'Don't you know when the fellow will be back? Haven't you any idea?'

'I didn't know he was out,' Arnold said. 'He doesn't go out much.' He added, slowly, 'I've never known him go out in the evening yet.'

'You mean . . .' the agent began. 'You mean he might be skulking inside there?'

'He might be.'

'If he is, I'll have him out.'

Arnold said, still more slowly and reluctantly:

'The back door'll be open.'

He had a sense of treachery. He didn't like to let an invader, any invader, into Cottontree House. It wasn't that he had any wish to protect Sonny. If there was trouble for Sonny it could come, and the more the better. But he didn't feel pleased with himself.

'Show me the way!' Mr Blackburn ordered him.

Arnold led the agent through the yard and in at the kitchen door. The kitchen was empty. It was getting dusky inside, but there didn't seem to be any lights on anywhere in the house. They walked round the ground floor, loose boards creaking occasionally under their feet.

'Shocking state this house is in,' the agent said.

Upstairs they looked in all the rooms except one at the back.

Arnold led the way past it towards the little staircase that went up to the attic. But the agent noticed.

'What's in that one?' he asked.

'Oh, that's my dad's. He's in bed, poorly.'

'I'll have a word with him.'

'I wouldn't if I was you,' Arnold said. 'I reckon he's asleep, or he'd have heard the noise and been calling to know what it was.'

'I'd like to have a look at old Ernest,' Mr Blackburn insisted. 'I've known Ernest Haithwaite these thirty years. He wouldn't like it if he heard I'd been here and not had a word with him.'

'All right.'

Arnold pushed open the door.

From where he was there was nothing to be seen at first but a shape under the bedclothes. But the smell, the sickroom smell, was unpleasant. Mr Blackburn pushed past Arnold, strode to the bed-head. Arnold followed. Ernest's face was sideways on the pillow. What you could see of it, under the grey stubble of an old man who hadn't been shaved for days, was hollow, whitish-yellow, repellent. Ernest's teeth, and the remains of a meal, were on the bedside table. He groaned, seemingly in his sleep.

The Duchy agent gave an exclamation of shock.

'This man's ill!' he said sharply. 'Desperately ill, if you ask me. Ring for the doctor at once, boy. Who's your doctor – is it Pearce of Irontown?'

Arnold nodded.

'You're not on the phone, I suppose? Well, run to the call-box, then ... No, wait a minute, I'll go. Pearce may be readier to turn out for me than he would for you.'

Arnold stepped aside. Mr Blackburn was out of the room in a moment. His footsteps sounded from the stairs, then there was the slam of the back door.

Arnold, shaken, looked down at the old man. Ernest's head turned on the pillow. He recognized Arnold. But there wasn't any pleasure of recognition. There was nothing in the old man's eyes but physical pain.

'I'm poorly,' he said. He turned aside again, his face screwed up. Sweat stood on his forehead. He groaned once more.

Arnold wondered if he should hold the old man's hand or wipe his brow, but he didn't want to. He was sorry for Ernest Haithwaite but he couldn't bear to touch him.

The old man's lips twisted. He seemed only just conscious.

'It's him,' he said. 'You was right. I should never have let him come.' His voice dropped to a mumble.

Then Arnold had the feeling he had had once before that Sonny was there, watching him. Something told him that movement would be dangerous. For a few seconds he stood quite still, looking down at the yellowy face of the old man. Then – very, very slowly, a millimetre at a time – he turned head and eyes towards the doorway.

The stranger's good eye met his. The man's left hand was by his side, clenching and unclenching. The right hand was behind his back. His voice was quiet, barely audible.

'You brought him in,' he said. 'I saw. I heard. I'm not a fool. I know who he is.'

'What have you done to my dad?' Arnold demanded.

'What have you done to me? Hindered me at every turn, that's what you've done. And now you've brought him in, brought him in through the back door. You want to destroy me and all my work. I know who he is.'

'Then why didn't you go down and speak to him, instead of hiding yourself away?' Arnold said.

Sonny flinched, and Arnold knew he had scored a hit. The man was afraid of the Duchy agent. Mr Blackburn represented power and tradition and authority. Sonny hadn't the kind of courage that stood up to power and tradition and authority.

'You're scared!' Arnold said, following up. 'You're not scared of a boy or an old man, but you're scared of him. Scared, scared, scared!'

Hate blazed in the good eye. Then the hand whipped out from behind the stranger's back. Something flew past Arnold's face. It was a heavy glass inkwell from the visitors' room. It crashed into the plaster and disappeared, leaving a jagged hole.

The stranger pounced. Arnold dodged round the bed. Sonny jumped across it. Arnold, on the man's blind side, reversed quickly and darted for the door. He was down the stairs in a couple of

166

perilous leaps. He lifted the catch on the front door, shot through it, and slammed it behind him in the stranger's face.

He was in the street. Wind hit him, and the rain sliced into his face from sideways on. He looked round in the hope of seeing Mr Blackburn, but there was no one there. He raced downhill towards the quay. At the near side of it was a track to the beach, used by children and dogs. Arnold turned sharply into it. The man saw him and followed. His footsteps, sounding from the pavement, were silenced as he left the street, and there was only the wind.

Once on the beach, Arnold was confident. He knew the bay, knew where it was safe to go and for how long. Carved by the river channels, swept by the wind into recurrent shapes, the estuary sands were never level. Arnold headed straight out from the shore towards a bank of higher sand that ran south of the river.

The sand was still firm, though with a slight softening underfoot that would have told Arnold, if he hadn't known, that the tide was coming. He was gaining on the man now. If he could get far enough ahead he could lose the stranger in the dusk, could follow the sandbank round to shore, higher up the Skirl.

But however well you knew the bay, you could only know it from one day to the next. A channel had changed its course since yesterday's tide. The sandbank was on the far side of several feet of fast-flowing water. Arnold glanced back. The stranger was twenty or thirty yards behind, and slightly to his right. There wasn't room to get round him without being headed off.

Arnold had no choice. He plunged into thigh-high water, waded through it, clambered up the unstable bank at the other side and was on firm ground again. Sonny followed, but lost time scrabbling up the cliff of collapsing sand. Arnold ran swiftly up-river, towards the viaduct. And after a minute he was stopped. The channels were changed again, and he was in the apex of an upturned V, formed where the river branched. Flowing towards him the Skirl was full, deep and fast, swollen with a week's rain on the western fells. He faced it for a second, panting deeply. It was a total barrier. Only one way was open. Arnold ran out towards the sea.

Now he had to get past the stranger. The man was running to cut him off. Arnold veered right, spurted, thought he could just get by. But as he raced past, Sonny flew from the ground, dived at his ankles in a superb Rugby tackle, and brought him down flat and breathless on his face.

Arnold was past fear now, and past hope too. The man who had twice wrestled with him and won easily, the man who had flung that heavy inkwell, could kill him and probably would. The man was beyond the reach of reason. And if Sonny didn't kill him the sea would do it soon. He waited. The minutes in which he could escape – might escape – were passing, and there were not many of them.

Nothing happened. The man had released his ankles and was crouching by him, not touching him. At first Arnold couldn't have moved if he had tried; knew that if he did move the man would pounce. Out here it was quiet. The wind could be felt but wasn't noisy, for there was nothing standing in its way.

A minute passed. Face down on the sand, Arnold could feel the coming tide throbbing through his body now. It was a mile away, most likely. But a mile was nothing here. The power of movement came back into him. Still without stirring, he wound himself up, tensed himself like elastic.

He bounded sideways. A split second would have got him away. But he didn't have a split second. The man grabbed him, brought him down, left him down. And then, again, nothing happened.

Slowly Arnold looked round. Sonny, motionless, was watching him with the good eye. When at last he spoke he seemed surprised, didn't appear to know why they were here or what they were doing. But clearly a thought was filling his mind.

'It's mine,' was all he said.

'What is?'

'The house. The Duchy lease. It's mine. I'm Arnold Haithwaite. You're nothing, you're from nowhere. Go back to nowhere.'

'I'm going,' Arnold said. 'Leaving Skirlston.'

'You may say so.' The man was suspicious. 'But you could come back. You could come back and try to take it from me. I won't have it taken. It's my house. It's property.'

'You're mad,' Arnold said. His voice rose. A body attuned to the bay since childhood was ringing now with the sound and power of the coming sea. 'In another minute we'll neither of us care any more, we'll be drowned.'

The man took no notice.

'It's family property,' he said. 'Mine.'

'Look!' said Arnold. He pointed out to sea.

There was nothing there. It was almost dark. But the stranger turned, to use his good eye. Arnold hit him, knocked him sideways and ran again.

He headed northward now. He knew he couldn't get back through the deep channel he had crossed at the Skirlston side. He hoped the wider, shallower channels between here and the Church in the Sea could still be waded.

He ran, and the sea was there. The first wave hit him, jolted him, passed by, was out of sight. And then there were no channels visible, only water. Water, one minute not there at all, next minute everywhere. Water round his knees and rising.

Arnold splashed on. Under his feet the sand crumbled and he was up to his waist. A channel. He waded. Then he was trying to climb, and step after step the bank was collapsing, letting him down again. It was like walking up a madman's staircase. Then a precarious firmness, a scramble, and the water was knee-high again. He hurried ahead as best he could. A quick look round showed Sonny, now barely visible in the gloom, but scrambling from the channel behind him.

Arnold waded another channel. The water surface swirled and eddied now as incoming and outgoing water met, danced, reared up, slid round each other. Under the surface, currents drew him all ways, nebulous arms twining round parts of his body, now gently persuading him, now jerking him viciously. For a moment his feet lost the bottom, moved sideways as if someone were trying to steal them from him. And then he was treading uphill again, was half-way out of the water.

Arnold thought he would die now. He knew Sonny would die.

Ahead, perhaps a quarter of a mile away, the shape of the church loomed through the dusk. Somewhere beyond it, lights were flashing. They made no sense to Arnold. He waded on, bent forward and sideways against wind and tide. A big wave came in, lifted him momentarily off his feet, splashed up into his face, and went past.

He felt the sand collapsing again, and knew he was on the brink of the last channel. He couldn't walk it. Common sense said he couldn't swim it either, for the water here was throwing itself all ways, inconstant in height and direction, insane with currents.

Common sense said he couldn't swim it, but if he didn't try he was a drowned man anyway. Arnold tore off his jacket, stretched his arms forward together, pushed himself off from the crumbling bank, struck out fiercely with the breast-stroke that was all he knew. The water was under and over and round him. He was above for a moment. The rush of a current carried him twenty feet. He struck out again and again, absurdly, inadequately, a frog in a torrent. He didn't know which way he was going. It was over and round him again, it was in his nose and mouth. His head came up, he gulped for air, took in water. He struck out again.

And he was on his feet, the sand rising under him, the sea no more than thigh-high, the waves passing him like pulses but still below his shoulders. He was out of the channel, the sand rising towards the north shore and the church and the causeway. Arnold choked, retched, waded on.

The rocks of the church island scraped his knees. He could hardly drag himself up. A high wave sprayed over him, threatening even now to pull him down. He crawled on over the slippery surface. He was on the island, though he couldn't see it. Under his feet was stone. Over them was water, just a little water.

Arnold looked back at last, scanned the dark heaving surface behind him. There was something that might have been a face back there. But it might have been a breaking wave, a momentary white crest in the gloom. He thought he heard a cry, long-drawn, desperate, dying to a gurgle, but in a night full of noise it could have been the wind, a gull, anything.

He splashed through the last few feet to the gaping doorway of the church, and his arms were full of Jane.

Chapter Twenty-seven

She was salty, sodden, terrified. They were both as wet as sea creatures. Arnold had never held her before, didn't feel as if he was holding her in any personal way now. But for the moment they were clasped together in the damp and noisy dark. She put her mouth to his ear.

'Is it high tide yet?' she asked.

Arnold's mind was still on Sonny.

'He's dead,' he said, half to himself.

'Has it turned, Arnold? You know all about it. Has it turned?'

'He's dead,' Arnold said. 'He must be.' He disengaged himself, went from the church doorway and looked out across the murky turbulence of the sea. The lights were on now in Skirlston, over the bay. It didn't seem to be raining, but the showers of spray were endless. There was no sign of Sonny. There couldn't be any sign of Sonny. He knew what had happened to Sonny.

'Arnold!' she called from behind him. She sounded frightened, as if he might leave her, which was absurd. 'Arnold, it hasn't turned, has it? It's still coming up. How much higher is it going to come?'

'He's dead. I didn't try to help him. But I couldn't. It was him or me, and maybe both of us.' Arnold still watched the sea. If by a miracle Sonny had appeared he would have helped him, would have risked everything to help him. Not heroically, not because he wanted the man to live, but because everyone was on the same side against the sea.

'Who's dead?' Jane said. The word had sunk in now. 'Who's dead?' Panic quickened her voice. It might have been Jeremy. It might have been Peter.

'Sonny,' he said in her ear. 'He chased me on to the sands. He can't be alive in that.'

172

'Oh, Sonny . . . Oh, how dreadful.' But in the present danger she wasn't really able to care about Sonny. She caught Arnold's arm.

'Come inside!' she begged him.

It wasn't safe out there, with the wind still blowing and the waves rolling past or breaking on the remains of the surrounding wall. And the stones underfoot were sloping and slippery. Arms linked, they retreated to the dark interior of the church. Then Jane asked once more:

'How much higher will it come?'

'I don't know. What time is it?'

Arnold's watch was waterlogged, but Jane's was working and had a luminous dial.

'Ten past eight,' she said.

Arnold felt a fresh surge of worry.

'Then it's quite a way to go,' he told her. 'You can't be sure in weather like this, but it could come up another six or eight feet, easy.'

'Enough to drown us?'

'Yes.'

She shuddered. He shouted into her ear:

'Don't worry. I've lost one tonight. I'm not losing any more.'

For the moment Jane was reassured. But Arnold wasn't as confident as he had tried to sound. Water was swirling round inside the church already, as if in an enormous bathtub. It poured in and drained out alternately through the open doorway, but always there was more coming in than going out, always the level was rising. Suppose you were a good swimmer like Jane – never mind being a poor swimmer like himself? Could you swim around in this as it got higher, or would it bounce you on the stone walls, bruise you, beat you into unconsciousness, drown you in the end? Would it be better just to stand, to brace yourself, to let it rise to chest, shoulder, chin, to go up on your toes . . .?

You couldn't talk in here, you could only shout, in competition with the reverberations of wind and sea. Jane put wet arms round Arnold's neck and yelled at him.

'What do we do now?' she was asking.

But he didn't know. What did you do, trapped in a stone tank with the water rising?

A stone tank. Stone walls. But not all stone. Somewhere in the back of his mind an image appeared, a fleeting image from years before. It was a picture of Ted Whiston, the council bricklayer, surrounded by children – Arnold one of them – and filling in the archway. The archway to the stumpy, useless tower. The stumpy, useless, dangerous tower.

People had been getting into the tower. Someone had been badly hurt by a fall on the narrow crumbling spiral staircase inside. Someone else had thrown himself from the top on to the stones below. And the council had sent Ted Whiston to brick the archway up.

Arnold concentrated hard, fine-tuning the image. The children had got in Ted's way and he had turned them off, but they had crept back. They had watched Ted laying course upon course of bricks, closing the gap. He had been pretty quick, and his work had been rough and ready. And surely it had only been one brick thick. And then the council had had it limewashed, along with the rest of the inside.

Well, it was a chance. Not much of a chance, but the only one. Arnold waded outside again. It seemed lighter there, in contrast to the darkness within. The sea was round and through and over the remnants of surrounding wall, throwing rocks about. Arnold picked one he could handle, carried it inside. A torch would have been handy, but neither of them had a torch.

He thought he could find the bricked-up opening easily, thought he could feel the difference of texture, thought he could tell a different tone if he hit it with the rock. But it was harder than he thought. Sound gave no guidance among tonight's orchestration of noise. Successive coats of limewash had lessened the surface difference between brick and stone.

Arnold groped and probed. Water licked round him, sending up sharp reminders of the lack of time. He bawled into Jane's ear, tried to tell her what he was up to, didn't know whether she understood or not. Then they were both groping, groping in the dark against the blank unyielding wall.

Jane had understood, and thought she had found the place. Arnold felt at it, wasn't sure. Sensitivity seemed by now to have worn away from his fingers. He hit the wall with the rock to see

174

what happened. Nothing moved, and his forearms were painfully jarred. He hit it two or three more times. Still nothing moved. He stood back, threw the rock at the wall at waist-height. It bounced and fell back. Water covered it.

'Something gave!' Jane cried. She was feeling again at the surface. Arnold didn't believe her. But he found the rock, retrieved it from the water, hurled it once more at the wall. Once more it bounced.

He was weary, didn't want to bother any more. He knew where the rock was, could kick it, did kick it, but couldn't bring himself to pick it up.

She was tugging at his arm.

'Again!' she shouted in his ear. 'Again!'

Arnold took up the rock. Strength came back, and with it a change of feeling, and he was suddenly furious. He was furious with the church and Ted Whiston's brickwork and the sea and the rock itself and all the things and people that had brought him to where he was. Heedless of the shaking it gave him, he battered away at the wall. He swore between blows, swore at the top of his voice, swore and hit, swore and hit.

And it was the brickwork he was hitting at, and it gave. It shifted under two successive blows, too quickly for Arnold's rhythm to change. At the third blow a bit of wall yielded, the rock left his hands and was gone. There was a ragged hole. There was Jane, feeling at its edges. There was Arnold standing empty-handed, not seeming to know what had happened, still swearing.

Jane tore at the bricks with her hands but couldn't move any more of them. Arnold tried and couldn't move them either. Nothing bigger than a cat could have got through the hole. He waded out, found another stone and battered afresh at the edges of the hole. More bricks fell back. The fury went out of Arnold. It had served its purpose. He stopped swearing. It was a dull, nagging battle now between him and the wall. He beat away, beat away. One side of the hole seemed fixed, immovable. The other gave, brick by brick. At last there was a gap that looked as if a person could squeeze through it. Arnold tried, and was stuck. He had a moment's panic, thinking himself trapped half-way through the wall. He drew himself back with a few scratches and went on attacking the edges of the hole. As it grew bigger the sea rose over its lower lip. Arnold tried again, forced himself through sideways, and was standing in what seemed like a cupboard. The sense of being in a narrow prison was overwhelming. But the air was breathable, and from far above came a thin gleam of light.

Arnold felt around for the remembered spiral stairway. There was nothing left of its bottom end but scattered stones, now under water. But from half a dozen steps up it was all there and apparently sound. Arnold leaped and clung, dragged himself on to the lowest remaining steps and wormed his way upward. The steps

were solidly based but their edges worn away, little more than toeholds. Twice he lost his grip and slithered backwards, the second time from several feet up. And then he had made it and was in some kind of small chamber at the roof level of the church. A slit was letting in that thin bar of light he had seen. There were more steps spiralling up into the tower itself, narrower and more peril-ous-looking still, but Arnold wasn't interested in them. He was sure he was now above any possible water-level.

Jane was calling to him through the hole. He hallooed loudly, then set off back to her, down the stairway. It was harder than going up. He probed at each step for a firm grip, shifting his weight cautiously, knowing he was lost if he slipped. Under him the sea lay in wait, swirling around in the narrow, black, coffin-like space. He jumped the missing steps and was at floor-level again, more than thigh-high in water. It was more than half-way up the hole he had made. Arnold leaned through, hooked his arms under Jane's, heaved and heaved, was dragging her through the hole, through water, through panic and despair and death and resurrection all in a second. And then she was upright and alive in his arms, choking and spluttering but alive.

Arnold bawled in her ear, trying again to tell her what she had to do. Then he was shoving her from underneath, shoving her up the spiral stairway, taking her weight until she had got a grip on the worn stone steps and was crawling away from him.

The sea was chest-high now. The hole into the church was closed and the sounds from the other side were blotted out. Here it was almost quiet, with just a thin wailing from somewhere in the tower above. Arnold groped once more for the steps, found where they began, but was weary. He scrabbled but couldn't get a grip, scrabbled again and again and still fell back. He lost his footing, and his head was under water and it was in his nose and mouth and he couldn't be bothered any more. And then his feet were on the ground and his head and shoulders were clear and he was scrabbling, scrabbling again.

Jane's voice came from above.

'Arnold! Are you all right? Arnold!'

He couldn't answer because he was half choked. But he leaped again, reached up with his hands and had a grip – a slight, sliding grip, but a grip, enough for him to press his body against the steps, to reach out wildly again and get a better hold. And then he was on his way up. And then he was in the little chamber and Jane was holding him and the water was below and it couldn't touch them.

They stood locked together, drenched, half conscious, coughing with the water they had swallowed.

'He's dead,' Arnold said when he could speak. 'Sonny's dead. He must be dead.'

It was minutes before either said anything more. Then Jane asked:

'Why did you come here, Arnold?'

'He was after me. He'd have killed me. I led him on to the sands. I knew what would happen, going on the sands a night like this.'

'Would he *really* have killed you?'

'Yes.'

'Then you can't blame yourself.'

Arnold hadn't the words to explain it to her. He would have hit Sonny in self-defence with anything that came to hand, he wouldn't have cared what happened. But it wasn't the same. He had led Sonny on to the sands and the sea had got him. No one who sought to be Sand Pilot should hand a man to the sea. For that there was no forgiveness.

'He might not be dead after all,' Jane said. The fear of death was something she had just learned, but the fact of death was still beyond her and she couldn't quite believe it. 'He'll probably turn up like a bad penny,' she said. 'Poor man.'

Arnold didn't answer.

'Anyway,' she went on, 'if you hadn't led him on to the sands you wouldn't have found *me*. And *I'd* have been drowned by now.'

She couldn't quite believe that, either. It wasn't possible for her to be dead. But she shuddered at her own words and clung to Arnold more closely, seeking and finding a trace of warmth through the soaked clothes of both of them. Suddenly she giggled.

'You *swore* your way through that wall,' she said. 'Fancy swearing through a stone wall.'

'A brick wall,' Arnold corrected her. Even in the cold and dark he felt his cheeks burn as he remembered the words he had used. 'Forget it,' he said.

'I'll never forget.'

'I'm sorry,' Arnold said. 'I suppose I'm rough ... I suppose Jeremy wouldn't have said all that.'

'Jeremy wouldn't have got through that wall, either.'

Arnold, still embarrassed, said nothing. But after a few minutes he asked:

'Is your watch going?'

'No,' she said. 'It stopped at twenty past eight.'

'I reckon the tide's turned,' said Arnold. 'I'm sure it has.'

'How do you know?'

'Well, it's a matter of time. It *must* have, by now. And I can sort of hear the difference, although a night like this you can't be sure.'

He went to the top of the little stairway and peered down into the dark.

'Careful, Arnold!' Jane called, a note of alarm in her voice.

'I'm always careful,' Arnold said.

He eased himself down the first few steps and, sitting, stretched out a cautious foot.

'It's no higher,' he said. 'Which means it must be going down.'

'And we're safe?' she asked.

'We were safe as soon as we got up here.'

'Well, we're *safer*.'

'You can't be safer than safe.'

'Don't be awkward, Arnold. And come away from that corner. I don't want anything to happen to you now. And can we sit down?'

The floor of the chamber was dry. They sat side by side, propped against the wall. Jane leaned against Arnold, her wet hair on his cheek. She drew his arm round her shoulder.

'We might as well be comfortable,' she said.

'He's dead,' said Arnold. 'He must be.'

Towards midnight the Admiral and Len Crowther and Jack Benson crossed the sands, roped together against the strong ebb of the River Skirl. They knew from Jeremy where Jane was. Inside the old church they found the hole that Arnold had made in Ted Whiston's wall. It was Len who clawed his way up the spiral staircase. He found Jane asleep, her head in Arnold's lap. Arnold sat as he had been before, back against the wall and legs stretched out. He stared straight ahead of him, awake but hardly interested in Len's arrival.

Len was facetious at all times.

'Fine place to take a young lady on a night like this,' he said.

'Sonny's dead,' said Arnold. 'He must be.'

Chapter Twenty-eight

Peter woke. It was half past nine, and a fine sunny morning. He put a dressing-gown on and went to the landing window that looked across the bay. The tide had gone out and come in again and it was another high one, but not spectacular. The church was once more surrounded and water lapped the causeway, but the wind had dropped. The sea was blue and harmless-looking.

He padded into Jane's room. She seemed to be asleep, her hair all over the pillow, still slightly wet. But she stirred as he went in, opened her eyes, and sat up suddenly.

'Well!' he said.

'Well.'

'Quite a night.'

'You can say that again.'

'Tell me.'

'Don't you know?'

'I know some. Tell me more.'

'Peter!' Helen Ellison's voice came up the stairs. 'Don't disturb Jane.'

Peter winked at his sister, went to the stair-head, called, 'No, Mother,' and returned.

'I was in the church,' Jane said. 'I was cut off. Arnold saved me. He found a way to a sort of little stone room above the tide.'

'You make it sound quite ordinary,' Peter said.

'Oh, it wasn't ordinary,' said Jane.

She didn't know how to describe it. The sea was still swirling round in the back of her mind, and her memory was full of jumbled scenes as if from a half-recalled film. No, it wasn't ordinary. But it wasn't simply out of the ordinary. It was so far from the ordinary that there was a sense in which it hadn't happened. It was a mad interlude, a nightmare, a product of delirium. Life was not that. Life was your own bedroom, and meals and clothes and pocket-money, and half-days spent shopping in Windermere, and going back to school next week, and sedate outings with Jeremy. Something horrible had been thrust into life and withdrawn, and she didn't want any more of it.

'For heaven's sake,' Peter said, 'tell me what happened. Tell me what it felt like.'

She didn't want to tell anyone what it felt like.

'Arnold was a hero, wasn't he?' said Peter.

'I suppose so,' she said. A phrase of her own came into her mind. 'He swore his way through a wall.'

'He what?'

'He found a bricked-up way from the church, and banged and swore at it and found a way through, and that was how we escaped.'

'It must have been powerful language,' Peter said.

'It was.' She shuddered, recalling the crude repetition, the crude accent. That had been dreadful, part of the nightmare. She could hardly believe she had giggled afterwards, had clung to Arnold. That couldn't have been her. That was somebody else, a character in the film that kept projecting itself in the corners of her mind.

'Well, I give up,' Peter said. 'The most exciting night of our lives, and I can't get anything out of you. How did you *feel* with the water rising all round you? How did you *feel* when Arnold appeared? How do you feel *now*?'

'Grateful, of course,' Jane said.

'Grateful!' Peter was on the verge of jeering at her. 'Then you'd better say thank you to him nicely before you go back to school.'

'Yes, I will, of course I will.'

A thought occurred to Jane.

'What happened to Jeremy?' she asked.

'He got away all right. Had a bit of a fright, though. The track from the causeway across the salt-flats was all under water, and his car engine stalled in the middle. He only just made it on foot to the main road. Heaven knows how they'll ever get the car right.'

'Oh, poor Jeremy!' said Jane, with feeling.

'He looked pretty sick about the whole thing when I saw him,'

Peter said. 'Not just the car. I suppose he felt he'd let you down.'

'But he didn't let me down!' Jane said. 'I let *him* down. It was my own silliness. It wasn't his fault at all, and there was nothing he could have done. And now I suppose Arnold gets covered in glory and Jeremy looks like the one who ran off and left me in the lurch. And really ... well, I know Arnold was wonderful, and he saved my life, and I won't forget it till my dying day, but still ... I mean, Jeremy's not a coward, and he must have thought I'd be quite safe on the island, and he'd have helped me if he could. And now his car's ruined and it's all my fault.'

She was ashamed of all the times she had been impatient with Jeremy.

'I wonder when we'll be seeing him,' she said.

'Pretty soon, I expect,' said Peter. 'Not having the car, he couldn't get home last night. So he slept here, and I suppose he'll be here still.'

'Oh, I am glad.' She was eager to see Jeremy, to make things right between them. She hadn't appreciated him at all.

'Off you go, Peter,' she said. 'I'm going to get dressed.'

'Mother will be cross if you get up now.'

'I don't care if she is. I want to talk to that poor boy.'

'You mean Jeremy?'

'Of course I mean Jeremy,' she said.

'You dad's all right,' said the Admiral, 'and you can stop worrying about him. He's in Irontown General Hospital, that's where he is, and should have been there long ago if you ask me. Like a skeleton, Fred Bateman said. Something very odd about it, I can tell you. That Sonny would've had a lot to answer for, if they'd found him.'

'There's no trace of him, then?' Arnold asked.

The Admiral shook his head.

'No one's seen anything yet. We've been waiting for you. And for the tide to go down.'

'He's dead. He must be dead.'

Arnold struggled from the Admiral's bed in the cottage on the hill. He was wearing the Admiral's shirt and underpants.

'Where's my things?' he demanded.

183

The Admiral threw them to him, warm from hanging on the fire-guard. Arnold changed.

'There'll be Fred Bateman round any minute in his car,' the Admiral said. 'I told him I'd have you up and ready for two o'clock. And I have done, eh? All we need to know is where we're going.'

'From where I saw Sonny last,' said Arnold, 'he'll be on Red Bank.'

'As far round as that?'

'We were well across the bay,' Arnold said.

'Fred can drive us there,' said the Admiral. 'That's him now, hooting outside.'

The policeman was turning his car round in front of the cottage. He stopped it, got out, tilted the passenger seat so that Arnold could get into the back. At the other side of the back seat was Miss Binns. She looked away from Arnold. She was wearing an old tweed coat and was without make-up. The crow's-feet showed beside her eyes, and her skin was dry, and you could see the faint hairs on her upper lip. She looked older today than she could be in reality.

Arnold sat beside her, saying nothing. The Admiral got in at the front.

'We reckon he'll be on Red Bank, Fred,' he said.

'You reckon right,' said the policeman. 'At least, I've just had a report that there's a body there, near the path from the viaduct.'

The Admiral said nothing. He was a talkative man as a rule, but he was subdued today. The car pulled up the hill out of Skirlston and headed left at the main road.

Fred Bateman drove with care. Branches were strewn over the road, and at one point several stones had fallen from a drystone wall. The policeman got out and moved them from the carriageway. A little farther along a pair of grown lambs were wandering on the verge. They scampered in panic ahead of the car, were overtaken and ran off bleating.

'The old railway viaduct's had it,' Fred Bateman said.

'Down?' the Admiral asked.

'Not down, but soon will be. They'll have to demolish it. Dangerous.'

Past the viaduct a footpath led down to Red Bank. The policeman drew off the road.

'You wait in the car, miss,' he said to Miss Binns. 'Someone'll come back for you if we find anything.'

The land on both sides of the path was red with iron ore, but the sands were scoured clean by the tide. There were tangled branches washed up in clumps. There was driftwood, seaweed, all kinds of debris.

It didn't take long to find Sonny. He lay sprawled on coarse grass, something washed up with the rest. He was fully dressed, still wearing shoes and jacket, but with one trouser leg ripped wide open. There was blood all over his face. Where the fixed eye had been, there was only a socket.

He was dead. They had known he would be dead.

'Well, there he is,' Fred Bateman said. 'No doubt about *him*. We could all identify him, any one of us.'

'You mean, we all know it's the man we've seen around,' the Admiral said. 'We still don't know who he is.'

'He's old Ernest Haithwaite's nephew, isn't he?' the policeman asked.

'His cousin's son,' said Arnold. 'That's what he claimed to be. I don't know who he was really. He was trying to get me out.'

Arnold didn't feel indignation any longer. He didn't feel pity either. He didn't care at all about Sonny. But he still had a deep sense of guilt. He had lost a man to the sea.

'Maybe the young lady can tell us,' the policeman suggested.

'I doubt if *she* knows,' said Arnold.

'I'll go and fetch her, anyroad,' said the Admiral.

Arnold wondered if he should have volunteered. He had younger legs than the Admiral's. But he didn't fancy the job of bringing Miss Binns down here. He said nothing.

'Meanwhile,' Fred Bateman said, 'let's see if he has any means of identification on him.'

He searched through the man's pockets. There was nothing in any of the outer ones but a handkerchief. But in the inside pocket of the jacket a wallet remained.

The policeman placed its contents neatly, item by item, on the handkerchief. There were half a dozen sodden pound notes. There was a railway time-table. There was a driving licence.

'That should tell us something if we can read it,' Fred Bateman said. He opened it, looked hard at Arnold who wasn't really attending, closed it and put it with the other things.

There was a health service card, too. The policeman looked at that and folded it without a further glance at Arnold.

Then there was a much-creased letter, very old, with a snapshot inside. This occupied the constable for two or three minutes. He glanced several times at the dead man's face. Then he said to Arnold:

'What was the name of old Ernest's cousin, that this chap claimed to be the son of?'

Arnold thought for a moment.

'It was Tom, I think,' he said. And, after another moment, 'Aye, it was Thomas Haithwaite. Died thirty years ago.'

'That's right,' said Fred Bateman. 'It's as clear as day, now. Not a shadow of doubt. This fellow was what he always said he was. Tom Haithwaite was his father.'

He looked Arnold full in the face.

'God knows who you are, lad,' he said, 'but this is Arnold Haithwaite. Arnold Haithwaite's dead.'

Miss Binns marched steadily down the path to the shore, several paces ahead of the Admiral. Her lips were thinly set. Her eyes were dry. She ignored the policeman, she ignored Arnold. She went to the body, knelt on the sand, kissed the dead man's face briefly, then stood up again.

'All right,' she said in a flat, steady voice. 'That's that.'

'Take your time, miss,' the policeman said. 'Maybe you'd like us to leave you for a minute or two?'

'You needn't bother,' said Miss Binns. 'There's no point. It makes no difference now. Poor Sonny. He never had much luck.'

Chapter Twenty-nine

'So!' said the Admiral. 'You lost a man. What's that in a lifetime? I've lost eleven. My grandfather lost thirty-three, all in one day. He begged and begged them to wait, but they wouldn't. They had to get to the Cumberland bank that night, they said. They never got there at all. I can see my grandpa now, sitting in that corner where you are, telling the tale. The tide came in with a west wind behind it that must have been twice what we had last night. It came in half an hour early, just one tidal wave, six foot high, moving like an express train. Thirty-four men, and only one lived to tell the tale. But did it stop my grandfather? It did not. He was out on the sands again next day.'

'It wasn't his fault,' said Arnold. 'This was my fault. I led him to it.'

The Admiral poured two glasses of home-brewed wine, pushed one across to Arnold, downed the other and refilled it.

'That fellow brought it on himself,' he said.

'But I knew,' said Arnold. 'I was trying to get away from him, but still, I knew.'

'Now listen, lad,' said the Admiral. 'I'm going to get impatient with you in a minute. This is no way to carry on. Did I say I've lost eleven? Well, I reckon I've saved fifty. Don't worry about the one you lost, don't give him another thought. Think of them you're going to save over the years. Sit down and write a note to Arch Rawson, telling him you're not going farming after all. And pick your life up where you left off.'

'How can I?' said Arnold. 'Nothing's the same.'

'Everything's the same.'

'Of course it's not. You were at the inquest. They buried him as Arnold Haithwaite. As for me, I'll never know, but most likely my father was a Cardiff seaman. I'm nobody at all, that's the truth of it. Arnold Haithwaite's dead.'

'Dead?' said the Admiral. He downed the second glass of home-brew. 'You look pretty healthy to me. *You're* Arnold Haithwaite, always were and always will be. There's only room for one of them in Skirlston, and it's you. You might as well get used to it again. And now sup up like a man, don't moan like a lad.'

The Admiral went to the window.

'There's someone out there now,' he said. 'They're all right for another hour, but still, we'd best keep an eye on them. Have a look through the telescope, Arnold lad. See if it's someone we know.'

Arnold swung the telescope, trained it on the sands, picked out the figures of a young man and a girl, walking side by side. Sunshine was reflected from the long bright hair of the girl. They were safely in reach of Skirlston Quay, and while he watched they turned round and headed back towards it.

'It's all right,' he reported to the Admiral. 'I saw who it was. Those two won't be caught unawares, never again.'

Chapter Thirty

Three years. Much happens in three years, even in Skirlston.

Ernest Haithwaite recovers and lives for two of them, weak but contented, telling his muddled stories of old days on the railway. He dies without a sound from heart failure, overnight, no trouble.

The Admiral retires. Arnold becomes Sand Pilot. He cannot be Admiral of the Port of Skirlston until he's twenty-one, so he must wait another two years for that. Then he will be the youngest Admiral in England, maybe in the world. This thought doesn't impress him.

Arnold is courting Norma, the eldest Benson. She is the only girl of his age in Skirlston. She is tired now of hanging round the Irontown cinema and snack-bar, and ready to settle. Arnold reckons it will be safest to marry one who is used to Skirlston, for an incomer might not stay.

The Windbrake power-station is finished and working. John Ellison is building another, somewhere on the South Coast. Peter has done brilliantly in his examinations, and hopes to go up to his father's old college at Cambridge in two years' time. Jane didn't master that Latin. She left school and took a year's secretarial course, and now lives with two other girls in a flat in Pimlico. She meets Jeremy sometimes, remembers Arnold, but will never see him again. No Ellison returns to Skirlston. Other families from Windbrake share the manor-house with Miss Hendry. She still plans to publish the journal of her ancestor the sea-captain. She never will.

Len Crowther makes enough money to buy a bigger business at Blackpool. You cannot get a car repaired in Skirlston now, or buy petrol, or hire a taxi. No new houses are built. Jack Benson takes some stones from an old one to make a pigsty. If you climb the hill, you can see the nuclear power-station in white concrete glory five miles down the coast, and the motorway sweeping round the side of Widow's Fell. You can't get on to the motorway from Skirlston. Skirlston folk don't want to.

Skirlston is dying, no doubt about it. Arnold may be the last Sand Pilot, may be the last Admiral. He never thinks about the possibility. The job will live while ever he does, and that is enough. There's a time-scale for people and a time-scale for things. On our scale, a lifetime is long and change comes slowly. On the other scale, a hundred years or a thousand years are nothing. Villages, power-stations, motorways are built and crumble in a blink.

On that scale, only the elements endure.

Sea, sand, stone, slate, sky.